Shatter with Words
Langston Hughes

by Margo Sorenson

Cover Photo: Bettmann Archives
Inside Illustrations: Dea Marks

For Jim, Jane, and Jill, whose
encouragement and enthusiasm mean so much.

For the A Better Chance Foundation
students of Edina, Minnesota, whose courage
in the face of overwhelming odds is an inspiration.

For Linda, who helped open my eyes.

For information, contact
Perfection Learning® Corporation,
1-800-831-4190,
1000 North Second Avenue, P.O. Box 500,
Logan, Iowa 51546-1099.
PB ISBN-10: 0-7891-2152-2 ISBN-13: 978-0-7891-2152-3
RLB ISBN-10: 0-7807-6786-1 ISBN-13: 978-0-7807-6786-7

10 11 12 13 14 15 PP 13 12 11 10 09 08

Contents

1

Poetry Stinks!

Aleesa slumped down in her desk. She made a face at the writing on the board. Where did Ms. Carter get such dumb ideas for projects? One of those stupid teacher workshops, no doubt. She sighed. Social studies was so boring.

Ms. Carter was making everyone in class do a social studies enrichment project. Aleesa frowned. She watched Ms. Carter begin writing ideas on the board in purple ink.

Enrichment. Yuck. She didn't want to get enriched. Unless she could spend it at the mall. And she was *in* a great depression. Just thinking about more schoolwork did that.

Aleesa stared ahead at Kenneth's back. She snorted. Of course, Kenneth probably couldn't wait to do the project. Kenneth was like that. He kept saying he had to keep his grades up for football.

Aleesa tapped her pencil on her desk. She wrinkled up her nose. Kenneth thought he was something special. Not to *her!*

Kenneth stared at the board. He frowned at the writing. Just what he needed. More junk to do. As if football practice and baby-sitting his little brother weren't enough.

"You'll all learn a lot from doing these projects together," Ms. Carter was saying to the class. She looked at everyone. "People tried to change America during the Great Depression. Writers, politicians, and even poets worked to change things. These projects will help you really get into that period in history."

Ms. Carter smiled. "You'll find out about change in history," she said. "Why does it happen? Who makes it happen?" She tapped on the board with the purple marker.

Kenneth winced. Carter always smiled like that. Her smile stopped just below her eyes. Carter would have made a good spy in a TV movie. Maybe even a killer. She had no heart. None at all. No mercy for her students. Who cared about change anyway? Everything changed sooner or later. So what?

As Ms. Carter rattled on, Aleesa rolled her eyes. She didn't want to get *into* any period in history. She just wanted to get *out* of social studies. Period. She frowned at the list Ms. Carter was writing on the board.

Oklahoma Dust Bowl Family Skit
Harlem Renaissance Black Poets' Session
New Deal Politicians' Meeting

It made Aleesa dizzy just reading the list. She shut her eyes. Besides, how could any of those people change anything?

Like poets, for instance. *They* could change history? Right. They just wrote words that rhymed. And they wrote for "hoity-toity" people too. People who drank tea out of china cups. Poets couldn't change anything. "Hunh," Aleesa snorted. And what was the Harlem whatever, anyway?

"Did you say something, Aleesa?" Ms. Carter's voice sliced through the air.

Aleesa snapped to attention. Uh-oh. She must have snorted pretty loudly. Now she'd get in even *more* trouble. Her mouth felt dry. She stared at Ms. Carter. What could she say to get herself out of this?

"Uh . . . uh . . . nothing, Ms. Carter," Aleesa stammered. She felt her face get hot. "I . . . ah . . . think I have to blow my nose," she mumbled. Aleesa sniffled to give Ms. Carter more proof.

In front of Aleesa, Kenneth grinned and shook his head. There went Aleesa again. Always getting herself into trouble. You'd think she'd put a plug in that mouth one of these days, he told himself. If someone else said some of the stuff she said, they'd be in big trouble.

Ms. Carter frowned. "Hmm," she said. She narrowed her eyes. But then she turned back to the board.

Whew! Aleesa thought. She felt her forehead bead up with cold sweat.

Kenneth rested his chin on his hands. He stared at the board. Everyone knew Aleesa had a smart mouth. So people just ignored what she said. She usually got away with it. She was even kind of funny sometimes.

Kenneth frowned. But what a slacker! Aleesa got out of doing work all the time. It was a miracle her grades were good enough to play basketball. Or to keep her grandma from grounding her for life.

Kenneth looked at Ms. Carter. She was still writing more projects on the board. He just hoped he wouldn't have to work with Aleesa for the project.

Kenneth held back a shudder. Getting a bad grade on a project like this could really mess up his grades. And he had to stay eligible for football.

Aleesa was trouble. She didn't care about grades. Not

much, anyway.

Suddenly, Ms. Carter wheeled around. "I just decided," she said. "I'm going to *assign* partners," she announced. "*And* topics."

Everyone in the class shifted uneasily. Aleesa could hear sighs and groans all over the room.

"And I'll begin with you, Aleesa," Ms. Carter said. "You're getting a cold—you say. So you should get started on this project right away. You may be absent later." A smirk danced around the corners of her mouth. "I wouldn't want you to turn in a late project."

Great, Aleesa thought. She tried to arrange her face to look calm. Who would Carter stick her with? Would it be Tyleene, her best friend? Nah. Whatever else Carter was, she wasn't stupid.

Kenneth felt his neck muscles tense up. Nuh-uh. Carter wouldn't do that to him, would she? She wouldn't pair him with Aleesa? No, no, no, he begged silently.

Ms. Carter spoke to Aleesa. "I'm going to pair you with Kenneth," she said with a smile. "You'll work well together." She turned to point at the board. "I'll assign you the Harlem Renaissance Poets," she added.

Kenneth shut his eyes for a second. Now Ms. Carter had really done it.

"But Ms. Carter!" Aleesa began. Her face scrunched up. "I . . . I don't even like poetry," she wailed. "It's for wimps and old ladies!" She slid down even lower in her desk.

"Yeah, Ms. Carter," Kenneth echoed. He frowned. "Let us at least pick our own partners. I want to work with someone like DeWayne." He could see DeWayne's grin across the classroom.

Ms. Carter sighed. All around the class, kids whispered. Some giggled.

"That's exactly why *I'm* assigning this time," Ms. Carter said. "You need to experience new ideas. You need to work with new people." A smile flitted across her face. "Change," she said.

Kenneth sighed. He slumped down in his desk.

Aleesa tightened her mouth. She scribbled on her paper. A little square. Over and over, until it was dark.

"And," Ms. Carter added with a glint in her eye, "you two had better get started." She looked at Aleesa. "With that bad cold, you'll need all the time you can get." She glanced at Kenneth. "Start today after school."

Kenneth rolled his eyes. Great. He didn't even get a break. What had he done to deserve this?

Ms. Carter faced the class. "I want you all to go to the University of California library to do your research. You'll find the best resources there."

Wonderful, Aleesa thought bitterly. She hated the University of California library. She'd gotten lost the last time she'd tried to use it. And some weirdo hippie guy had popped out of the stacks of books. He'd scared her to death. All the college kids stared at her. Besides, there were just too many books there.

Kenneth rested his chin on his hands. The Cal library. It was okay. It was just hard to find stuff. Wait. He almost snickered. Maybe he could lose Aleesa in the stacks.

Ms. Carter's voice droned on. She assigned everyone a partner.

RRRRRIIIIIINNNGGGG! Finally! Aleesa thought. Class was over!

"Class dismissed," Ms. Carter said.

"All right," Kenneth said to Aleesa. He picked up his books. He shoved them into his backpack. "Let's get this over with. Let's get to the library. I've got other homework." He looked at her. "I bet you do too. But you probably won't do it," he said grinning.

"Be quiet," Aleesa pouted. She dropped her books in the bottom of her backpack with a thud. "What do *you* know, anyway?"

Kenneth and Aleesa pushed their way through the crowded halls. They walked outside into the late afternoon California sun. Kenneth hurried ahead.

"Hey!" Aleesa called out to his back. "Wait for me. This isn't a sprint test, you know," she grumbled.

"Well, hurry up," Kenneth said. He frowned as he waited on the crowded sidewalk. Together, they crossed University Avenue. He looked around at the crowded university campus. People walked everywhere. Kenneth and Aleesa hurried through Sather Gate and across Dwinelle Plaza.

"Okay, here's the library," Kenneth said. He started up the steps.

"As if I didn't know," Aleesa complained. "Why do you have to act like you know everything? You *don't,* you know."

They walked inside the double doors. Everywhere he looked were books, Kenneth thought. People were reading books. People were taking notes on what they read in books. People were talking about books.

"Let's get to a computer," Kenneth suggested. He slung his backpack over his shoulder. A row of computers sat on a table.

"Harlem what?" Aleesa asked, clicking the cursor. Then she reached for her backpack. She rustled around inside it. "I can't find my notes."

"Here," Kenneth said in disgust. He handed her a sheet of paper. "Harlem Renaissance. Remember? All the African American writers? The African American poets?"

Aleesa tapped in the words. "Whoa!" she exclaimed. "Look at all the people's names."

"Oh, yeah," Kenneth said. He leaned closer to the screen. He scanned the list of names. "I remember reading about some of these people in our textbook." He glanced at Aleesa. "Some of their poems too. Just like you read, I bet," he teased.

Aleesa tossed her head. "Maybe I did," she snapped. "It's none of your business." She scrolled the cursor down. "So pick one, smart man," she said.

"Langston Hughes," Kenneth said. "He was an African American poet. I remember some stuff about him. He wrote poetry that everyone could understand. I even liked one that I read in the book. I think it was called 'Life Is Fine.' It said that even if really bad things happen to you, life can still be fine. It made me think, anyway."

Kenneth looked at Aleesa. She probably wasn't even listening, he thought. "Let's copy down some of the call numbers," he suggested.

Aleesa finished jotting down numbers. She turned away from the computer. "Let's go," she said. "Eight-eleven and stuff like that."

They threaded their way through the library. Aleesa sniffed. "It smells like old dust in here," she complained.

"Sure that's not just your cold?" Kenneth mocked. His shoulders shook with laughter.

"Ha, ha," Aleesa snapped. They stopped in front of a section of shelves. Aleesa knelt down. "Here," she said. "Holy cow. There are tons of books by Langston Hughes. What was he? Famous or something?" she asked.

"One of the best poets ever," Kenneth said. He leaned an elbow on a shelf.

CRASH! THUD! BAM! A dozen books toppled over from the top shelf.

"Ow!" Aleesa howled. She rubbed her head. She scrunched up her face. "Thanks, creep," she said. Shining splotches came and went behind her closed eyelids. "Ouch!"

"Aaaargh!" Kenneth exclaimed. He rubbed his head too. "They got me too. It hurt." He was having a hard time seeing, he realized. Things were kind of blurry.

"No kidding," Aleesa snapped. "And I'm dizzy too." She began to reach into her backpack for some tissues. Aleesa stopped. Her backpack was gone. She looked down at her clothes. And what was she wearing? What happened to her jeans? She was wearing some weird-looking long dress! Her heart almost stopped. She whipped around to look at Kenneth.

"Kenneth!" Aleesa said hoarsely. "Look at you!"

Kenneth looked down. He was wearing some strange outfit—like a tan suit or something. And his collar was tight around his neck. And—he had on a tie! What was Aleesa wearing? A weird old-fashioned dress? His head pounded. He shook it, trying to clear it.

"S-something's not right. What—what happened to us?" Kenneth managed to choke out.

2

Back in Time

Aleesa looked around in a daze. Her jaw dropped. "Hey," she whispered. "Everyone else is dressed like us!" She pointed to other students looking at books on the shelves.

Kenneth swallowed hard. "You're right," he admitted. He noticed something else about the students.

"And look at their hair. Freaky. Like old-fashioned," he added.

Aleesa began to giggle. "And you think yours looks *different?*" she asked. She leaned against the shelf in helpless laughter.

Kenneth felt the top of his head. "Oh, man!" he exclaimed. "What's up with this?" Then he stared at Aleesa. "Nice bob," he commented.

Aleesa's eyes widened. She reached up and touched her hair. "What?" she almost screeched. "I must look like one of those old-time pictures in our textbook!" Then her forehead creased with worry. "What's happened to us? What's wrong? I—I want to go home," she begged. "Even to listen to Grandma nag me. This is giving me the creeps. Let's just get out of here and hope we don't see anybody we know."

"Good idea," Kenneth agreed. He picked up his books. His hands shook a little. Something was definitely wrong here. He and Aleesa began walking through the rows of shelves. The librarians' desks sat next to the entrance.

Aleesa stopped. She turned her worried face to Kenneth. "You know what?" she asked slowly. "This doesn't look like the university library anymore." She peered around her. "It—it looks different somehow. It's a library. But it's not Berkeley. I don't think," she finished in a whisper.

Kenneth stopped next to her. He looked around. "You're right," he said slowly. "It's a lot smaller. That's for sure. I don't recognize anything either."

"As if you spent your life in here, you geek," Aleesa teased. But then something caught her eye. She swallowed hard. "Kenneth," she whispered. She pointed above the librarians' desks. "Look at the calendar on the wall." Her finger shook. "Look at that!"

A prickle of fear ran down Kenneth's spine. "This has got to be a joke," he said. "November 1931?" In a panic, he looked around. "Okay. This has got to be one of those TV shows, you know?" he blustered. "Where they have the hidden camera? And when you say and do dumb stuff—and you're on national TV?"

Aleesa shivered a little. "Shhhh!" she whispered. "I—I don't think so. It's too perfect. And besides," she added. "Look at the sign." She pointed at the wall.

"Virginia Union College Founders' Library?" Kenneth said, reading the words. "We're in Virginia? In 1931? Uh—" he began. Then he stopped. "If that's true—" He stopped and swallowed hard. "We—ah—could be in a little trouble here."

Kenneth's mouth felt dry. He clenched his fists. Maybe it was a trick. Someone was setting them up. Maybe DeWayne and his football buddies.

Then, a feeling of dread began to creep through him. What if they really *were* here? What if they were stuck here?

"What do you mean?" Aleesa asked. She took a step toward Kenneth.

Kenneth fought a rising tide of panic. He bent his head down to Aleesa. "Listen. If we're really here, we're in trouble. *Big* trouble. We're in the South, Aleesa. Before the Civil Rights Movement and all that stuff. Do you get what I mean?" he asked.

"Well," Aleesa began. She looked around them. "But everyone else in here is African American too," she said. She looked at Kenneth's serious face. Then her eyes grew huge in her face. "Oh, no! You mean—like before Dr. Martin Luther King?" A current of fear ran through her. "Kenneth—this is scary!" she said. "I want to go home! Right now!" she wailed softly.

"Me too," Kenneth admitted. Then he straightened his shoulders. Coach would tell him to be tough. So would Mom. Aleesa was depending on him, whether he liked it or not. He cleared his throat.

"Look, Aleesa," Kenneth said in a low voice. "We've got to be careful." He looked around him. No one was paying attention to them. "We've got to figure out what's going on. But we can't let anyone find out who we are." He glanced over his shoulder again. "Or where we're from. They'll think we're crazy. And African Americans had it bad enough in the South in 1931. We'll have to find out how we can get home." If we even can, he added silently.

Aleesa's eyes filled with tears. "Kenneth!" she whispered. "I can't take this! I want to go home *now!*"

Kenneth grabbed her arm. "Shhhh!" he exclaimed. He glanced around. All three of the librarians looked up.

Two of them frowned at him. One put her finger across her lips.

The third librarian got up. She began walking toward them. Kenneth froze. Now what? Think! he commanded himself. Stay cool.

The librarian's face relaxed into a smile. "Are you kids here for the Langston Hughes poetry reading in an hour?" she asked.

Aleesa felt the blood drain from her face. "Langston Hughes?" she burst out. "But he's d—"

Kenneth squeezed her arm. "What she wants to say is that he's the best." He thought for sure the librarian could hear his head pounding in time with his heart. Langston Hughes! he repeated silently. They really were back in 1931.

"Yes. We certainly think so." The librarian smiled at them. "You've heard of his poetry then?" she asked.

Aleesa's face fell. She looked at Kenneth. Please, say something! she urged him silently.

"Uh . . . uh . . . yeah," Kenneth stammered. He took a ragged breath.

"Hmmm," the librarian said. "You must read a lot. He's a fairly new poet."

What had he done now? Kenneth wondered. He caught Aleesa looking daggers at him. He frowned at her. But the librarian went on talking.

"Not many people in the South know much about him," she continued. "Except that he writes for us—

Negroes. Not just for whites. He writes for regular people, not only educated Negroes. And he writes about our real lives. He's the first Negro poet to do that," she said.

Negro? Why was this woman using the word "Negro"? Aleesa almost squawked aloud. Then she remembered. That's what African Americans called themselves in 1931. Or—now. She swallowed hard. Good thing she didn't say anything.

"That's one reason he's doing this poetry-reading tour," the librarian explained. "His friend, the college president Mary McLeod Bethune, told him to 'take the poetry to the Negro people in the South.' And so he is.

"If you're done looking at books," the librarian went on, "why don't you come on and sit in the hall? I think he's already setting up." She looked down the hall. Then she motioned to them. Aleesa and Kenneth followed.

Now what? Aleesa asked herself. Her heart pounded with each step she took. They really must be in 1931. They were really going to hear this poet guy talk? Langston Hughes? She crinkled her forehead. She guessed she remembered Ms. Carter saying his name. But she sure didn't read the chapter.

Walking next to her, Kenneth kept looking around them. Was there a way to get back to their own time? Back to Berkeley, California? Would he see a secret door marked "Kenneth and Aleesa, open this?" His heart thudded.

This was like a bad dream. That was it! Maybe they were just dreaming. They'd wake up soon. Those books had knocked them out or something. He pinched himself. Ouch! Nope. They weren't asleep.

The librarian opened the double doors to the hall. "Here," she said, smiling at them.

Kenneth saw dozens of chairs lined up in rows, facing the front. Two young men, their backs to the door, were unpacking boxes of books.

"That's Mr. Hughes right there," the librarian whispered. "And his friend and driver, Radcliffe Lucas. Why don't you see if you can help them?" she suggested. "I have to get back to work," she finished. She left, shutting the double doors behind her with a click.

"Meet Langston Hughes?" Aleesa squeaked. "Are you kidding?" She hung back behind Kenneth.

Kenneth stared at the two young men. "I can't believe it," he said. "We're really going to meet Langston Hughes. Wait until Ms. Carter—" Then he stopped. What if they never saw Ms. Carter again?

The two young men turned around. They smiled. "Two eager young fans already?" the shorter one asked. "We could use some help," he said. "Can you help us unpack some of my poetry books? And some of these other books by Negro writers?"

Help Langston Hughes? Kenneth said to himself in a daze. Aleesa jabbed him with her elbow. He glared at her. "Uh . . . uh . . . yeah, sure," he said. He grabbed Aleesa's arm. Together, they walked down the center aisle between the rows of chairs.

What in the world was she doing? Aleesa asked herself. She didn't even *like* poetry. Poetry didn't have anything to do with her at all. And here she was, talking to a real poet. And a famous one too. Or so Kenneth said. And he always knew everything, she snorted silently. Of course.

The shorter young man stuck out his hand. "I'm Langston Hughes," he said grinning. Kenneth shook his hand. Aleesa did too.

"I'm . . . uh . . . Kenneth Smith," Kenneth stammered. He looked at Aleesa. Her mouth was open. She was staring at Langston. "And this is . . . uh . . . my friend Aleesa Strong," he added. "She's out of it. As usual," he joked. Aleesa made a face at him.

Langston threw his head back and laughed. "I hope she's *still* your friend," he said. "After that comment." He motioned to his friend. "This is my friend and my driver," he said. "Radcliffe Lucas. I don't have a license," he added. Kenneth and Aleesa shook hands with Radcliffe.

"Can you help us set these books up on the table?" Langston asked. "Some of them are by famous Negro writers. But they're just to look at. We're trying to show everyone in the South what Negro writers are publishing. And then there are my poetry books. We want to sell them." He grinned wryly. "We have to sell a lot. We'll go broke on this speaking tour if we don't," he added.

"What do you mean?" Aleesa asked. "Don't you poet guys make big money?"

"Big money?" Langston asked. He began to laugh

hard. He slapped his knee. Radcliffe joined in.

Their laughter was catching, Kenneth thought. Even though he didn't get it. He began to chuckle too. But Aleesa stood, her hand on her hip. What's so funny? she wondered.

"This is the Depression, remember?" Langston asked. "No one has money these days. And poets never make much money anyway. Sometimes I even do these readings for free," he said. He sighed and shook his head. "Especially if the college or church says they really can't afford to pay me. So I don't charge them anything. I just want to bring my poetry to the people. After all, I wrote it for them."

See? Kenneth wanted to tell Aleesa. He was right about Langston Hughes. He was a good guy.

"So I want them to hear it," Langston went on. "And lots of times, they'll buy one of my books. Or a pamphlet. They cost just a dollar."

Curious, Aleesa picked up one of the slim books. "The Weary Blues," she read aloud from the cover. "Sounds kind of good," she said. Even for poetry, she wanted to add. But she bit her tongue.

She opened to a page. She read silently for a few moments. The words seemed to reach out from the page. A strange feeling took hold of her. Words and images blended together in a wave of remembering. Langston's words almost burned in her mind. In awe, she slowly closed the book.

"This—this is really good!" she exclaimed. "I like

how you make the poetry sound like the blues," she said, looking at Langston. "I can really see that man play the piano. I can hear the rhythm," she said. "And it makes me feel sad and happy at the same time." She smiled in amazement. "How do you do that?" she asked.

Radcliffe answered. "Langston uses the blues for the rhythm of the words. He writes about our real lives."

"Okay, okay," Langston said grinning. "Radcliffe thinks he's my agent, not just my friend." Then Langston's grin faded. "Of course, some people don't like my poetry. Just because I write about everyday things. And because I write like how we talk sometimes. Hah! They think it's 'low-class.' Hmph!" he snorted. "Poetry is for real people—everybody. Not just the educated."

"If all your poetry is like this, no wonder you're so famous and in textbooks," Aleesa blurted out.

Langston and Radcliffe stared at her. "Famous?" Langston asked. "Textbooks?"

Kenneth jabbed her with his elbow. What trouble would Aleesa get them into now?

3
Should We Go?

Kenneth's forehead broke out in a cold sweat. Think!
he told himself. Langston and Radcliffe were still staring
at Aleesa.

Aleesa felt her face flush. Now she'd really done it.
What were they going to do?

"Uh . . . she means that someday you'll be in a

textbook," Kenneth said quickly. "Because your poetry's so good." He held his breath, watching their faces.

Langston suddenly grinned. "It's great to have fans," he said with a chuckle. "Well, fans, let's finish up here," he said.

Aleesa and Kenneth exchanged glances. Whew, Kenneth mouthed silently. Aleesa rolled her eyes. When they both bent over a box at the same time, Kenneth leaned closer to her.

"Now will you keep that big mouth shut for once?" he scolded in a low voice. "You almost got us in big trouble."

"You mind your own business," Aleesa snarled. "You're not so smart yourself."

They stacked books on the table. Radcliffe and Langston set up a microphone.

"Say," Langston said when they'd finished. "You two are a big help." He looked at them. "Would you two like to travel with us?" he asked. He leaned against the table. "Just for a couple of weeks? Until we get the hang of this.

"Radcliffe and I could use the help," he continued. "We have to do everything ourselves. I don't have much time to practice." He shook his head. "I hardly have time to think about which poems I'm going to read. And I'm not getting much poetry writing done."

"Each audience is a little different," Radcliffe explained. "Langston can't always read the same things."

"If I'm going to get my poetry to the people the way I want to, I could use some help," Langston explained.

Then he smiled again. "And if I'm going to make enough money to eat, I have to turn poetry into bread. So, what do you think?"

Thoughts flashed through Kenneth's head. Go along with Langston Hughes? Kenneth asked himself. It would be the experience of a lifetime! But should they leave the safety of the library? That might be their key to getting home. Then he frowned. But then—they couldn't sleep in the library, could they? And how would they eat?

A little twinge of fear ran through Kenneth. It could be dangerous here in the South by themselves. He frowned. They didn't have much of a choice. They'd better go with Langston until they figured out how to get home.

Hadn't Langston lived until he was an old man? Nothing had happened to him on the tour, had it? They should be safe then. It'd be safer than staying here by themselves, wouldn't it?

"N—no!" Aleesa blurted out. Kenneth stepped on her foot. "Ouch!" she squeaked. She glared at Kenneth. She leaned down and rubbed her aching toes.

"What did you say?" Langston asked. He looked puzzled.

"She means," Kenneth explained quickly. "We have to check with our school first. And our parents. But I'm sure they'll let us go."

If only they *could* check with their parents, he thought. How he wished he could check with Mom.

Would he and Aleesa ever see their families again?

"I thought you looked kind of young for college students," Langston commented. "Of course, I didn't finish college until last year. I'm 28 now. I just wasn't ready."

"No, but you'd already published lots of poems by then," Radcliffe said. "People already knew about you when you went to college."

"That's enough of that," Langston said modestly. "So, you'll find out and let me know?" he asked Kenneth and Aleesa. "Tomorrow? We're leaving for Virginia State College in the morning."

Kenneth and Aleesa stared at each other. Where would they stay the night? Aleesa wondered. What were they going to do?

Kenneth felt his muscles tense. He had to think of something.

"Ah—I'll give them a call right now," Kenneth said. "They'll probably let us go with you tonight," he added. He hoped this would work. Maybe they could stay with Langston and Radcliffe.

What else could they do about where to sleep tonight? He didn't want to sleep on any park bench. With all the Jim Crow laws about colored and white this and that? Drinking fountains? Doors? Restaurants? All that junk going on? No park bench for him. Not in the South in 1931. Not anywhere—ever. He held back a shudder.

"Oh, sure," Langston said. "You've got agreeable parents, I guess," he added smiling.

Should We Go?

"My grandma's a big poetry fan," Aleesa said quickly. Well, she was pretty sure Grandma would know who Langston Hughes was. Grandma knew all that stuff. She subscribed to the NAACP's magazine *The Crisis* and everything.

Langston and Radcliffe looked at each other and smiled. "Looks like we've got a couple of helpers," Radcliffe said. "Hope you kids don't mind sitting with boxes of books in the back seat of the old Ford."

"No problem," Kenneth assured him. He looked at Langston. "How much time do we have before your program? We'd like to—ah—call our families," he said. "To check," he added.

Aleesa stared at him. Kenneth wasn't really thinking of doing this, was he? Travel through the South before Civil Rights? Was he crazy or something? She didn't want to die.

Langston glanced at the clock on the wall. "About half an hour," he said. "Plenty of time."

"See you then," Kenneth said. He grabbed Aleesa's arm and began walking toward the double doors at the back of the hall.

"What are you thinking?" Aleesa hissed. She jerked her arm away from Kenneth. "Are you stupid? *You're* the one who reminded me about what the South was like for African Americans in the 1930s. Now you want to travel through it?" She shook her head in amazement. "I don't believe you," she said in disgust.

The double doors whooshed shut behind them. Kenneth saw a pay phone in the corridor. He took a quarter from his pocket. "Whew," he said. "Good thing I have some money." He dropped the coin in. He picked up the receiver.

"Just a second," Aleesa snapped at him. "Who do you think you're calling? Your mom isn't even born yet."

Two coins chinked down into the coin return. "Your call costs only a nickel," an operator's voice said into Kenneth's ear.

Kenneth stood holding the receiver to his ear. With his free hand, he scooped the coins out. He frowned at Aleesa. "Shhhhh," he said in a low voice. "What do you think I'm doing, dummy?" He shook his head. "Did you think about where you might have to sleep tonight? At least if we're with Langston, we'll have a place to stay. I'm not sleeping on any park bench. Not me. Nuh-uh. I want to be alive to see the sunrise."

Kenneth pretended to dial. "Mom?" he began. "Yeah, this is Kenneth . . ."

While Kenneth yapped, pretending to talk to his mom, Aleesa leaned against the wall. Her shoulders slumped. Kenneth was right, dang it. They didn't have anywhere to sleep tonight. They had to go with Langston, no matter what.

But how would they ever get back home? Aleesa shut her eyes. They couldn't stay in the library. Could they tell Langston their problem? Would he help them? Would he believe them? she wondered. Then she sighed and thumped her palms against the cool concrete wall. They were stuck, no matter what. Until they figured something out.

"Okay, let's go back," Kenneth said. "We'll tell them we got permission. But just for two weeks." He winked at her. "That ought to give us time to figure out how to get home. And if we're with Langston Hughes, we ought to be pretty safe. I hope."

Loud voices echoed down the corridor. Kenneth and Aleesa turned and watched. People were beginning to arrive. Four young African American men walked past them. One of them was really angry.

"I'm telling you, we never got treated like this in the North!" the tallest young man was arguing. He shook his fist. "Southerners are *unbelievable!*"

One of the young man's friends put a hand on his arm. "Come on, Chauncey. You knew it would be tough. You knew going on tour and playing the blues in the South wouldn't be easy."

"Yeah, Chauncey," another young man added. "Ralph's right. It's kind of late. And a lot of people are coming to hear us play the blues."

"And they like us, man," the fourth young man said. "Like Paul just said. In Detroit, we're cool. But folks like us even better here."

"They must be a blues band," Aleesa whispered to Kenneth. She watched the young men standing in the hall outside the double doors.

"Duh," Kenneth whispered back. Aleesa made a face at him.

Chauncey shrugged. "Fine. Say what you want. But I'm not gonna put up with this kind of junk much longer," he vowed, frowning.

"You'd better listen carefully to Langston then," Ralph urged. "He's got some good ideas. He wants change, too, for our people. But he's got a different way to do it."

"There's only one way to change this kind of treatment," Chauncey muttered. "I'll just break my guitar over someone's head. Break some bones. That's how."

"Be quiet, man," Ralph urged. He looked around them. "You can't go talking like that here in the South. I want you to pay attention to what Langston says."

"Yeah?" Chauncey retorted. "What would Langston say about that Negro football coach from Normal? The same guy who used to be a football star at Virginia State? Huh? He was just beaten to death. Not a couple hundred miles from here. Why? Because he parked his car in a "whites only" parking lot for the football game. He was early to meet his team. So he didn't even know he was in the wrong lot." Chauncey spit into a spittoon.

Ralph and the others looked at each other. Then they looked down at the ground.

Aleesa's mouth opened. This was awful. This was much worse than reading about it in a textbook. And Virginia State, Chauncey had said. That was where

Langston said they were going next, wasn't it? She glanced at Kenneth. He looked pale.

"And what about Juliette Derricote? Another one of our people. The Dean of Women at Fisk? I heard on the radio today. She just died too. And why?" Chauncey's voice rose. "Because she was in a car accident. And she didn't die in the car accident. No, sir. She died because a white hospital wouldn't treat her. That's why she died!"

Ralph took Chauncey's arm. "We know, man. We know. It ain't right. Langston Hughes knows it ain't right. But he's here speaking. He's here with a message. His poetry is the message. So let's listen."

The double doors opened. The four young men walked inside.

Kenneth and Aleesa looked at each other. Her face twisted with worry.

"Are you sure we're doing the right thing?" Aleesa asked him.

4

Words That Move

Kenneth shut his eyes for a second. Then he looked at
Aleesa. "Look," he said. He hoped he sounded braver
than he felt. "We don't have a choice. Just as I said. We
have to travel with Langston Hughes. We've got to have
some safety. We need time to figure out how to get home.
We need time to figure out how to get home.
And we have to stay out of trouble in the meantime. If
we're with Langston, we have a chance."

Aleesa sighed. She nodded her head slowly. "Yeah, I guess you're right," she admitted.

Aleesa watched the blues band take some seats near the front. Chauncey and Ralph got up to look at the poetry books on the table. They began turning the pages.

"So, you read the social studies chapter. Do you remember what happened to Langston Hughes during the tour?" Aleesa asked Kenneth. "He didn't get killed or anything, did he? Will anything happen to us?" she asked. She twisted her hands together.

Kenneth pressed his mouth together in a thin line. He shook his head. "I think Langston Hughes lived to be an old man," he said. "So we should be safe."

"But what about that football coach?" Aleesa said. Her voice rose a little higher. "Beaten to death. And that lady? That university dean they wouldn't even let into the hospital? So she died?" Aleesa drew a quivering breath. "That's so unfair," she said. "That's wrong. That's absolutely wrong. Thank goodness things have changed," she added.

"I know," Kenneth muttered. He glanced inside at the blues group. That guy they called Chauncey had gotten really angry about it too. Ralph had tried to calm him down.

"What was it that Ralph in the blues band said? Remember? About Langston Hughes?" Kenneth asked. "Didn't he say Langston had an idea on how to handle all of this junk?" He looked at Aleesa.

Aleesa nodded. "Yeah, he did." She took a deep breath.

"Well, Langston is *here,* isn't he? I mean, he's touring in the South. So Langston must think he'll be all right. And Ralph said Langston had a message in his poetry for the people. So let's hear what it is," Kenneth said. "It'll be all right."

Kenneth sure *hoped* everything would turn out all right. He shoved his hands into his pockets.

More and more African Americans crowded into the hall. Kenneth and Aleesa hurried in. They took seats right behind the blues band.

The audience was cheerful. People talked and greeted each other. Everyone seemed to know everyone else, Aleesa thought.

"I've been waiting for weeks for this!" a woman next to Aleesa said to her neighbor.

"So have I. I've been reading Langston Hughes's poems in *The Crisis,*" the other woman answered.

"He makes me laugh and cry at the same time," the first woman said. She shook her head, smiling.

' "That's because he writes about what we know about," the second woman replied. "I think he's a genius."

Then a man got up and stood behind the microphone.

"Ladies and gentlemen, it is my pleasure to introduce Langston Hughes, a speaker for our people. A writer of and for our people," he said. "Mr. Hughes has broken new ground with his poetry. He hasn't been afraid to write about what our lives are really like. Happy, yet miserable. Sad, but triumphant. Always confronting the evil around us with a spirit of hope and courage." The man paused and gazed out at the audience. A hush settled over the crowd.

"And Langston Hughes says," the man went on, "because of his poetry, he hopes to make everyone think. Everyone. And once you get people thinking, Langston Hughes says, then you can get change. So, without further ado, I present Langston Hughes—a poet for America."

The audience clapped loudly. Some people cheered.

Change, Kenneth thought. Wasn't that what Ms. Carter had said to find out about? How the Harlem Renaissance poets had helped America change? So that's what Langston Hughes was doing.

Kenneth sat up straighter in his chair. He'd better pay attention.

Langston got up and stood behind the microphone. He smiled at everyone.

"I'd like to open with a group of poems that I call 'Life Makes Poems,' " Langston said, beginning to read.

Aleesa sat riveted. Titles, words, and images crowded her mind. The magic of Langston Hughes's words pulled at her. The way he said the words aloud made her want to move in time with them.

When Langston finished with "Song for a Banjo Dance," Aleesa wanted to jump to her feet and clap hard. She looked at Kenneth as they both got up and clapped. Everyone else was standing and clapping too.

"He's amazing!" Aleesa said. Her eyes shone with excitement. "I didn't know poetry could be like this!"

"I told you," Kenneth said. He grinned.

Kenneth wondered if Langston would read "Life Is Fine." That was Kenneth's favorite. Uh-oh. What if Langston hadn't even written it yet? He'd better not say anything. That could get them into trouble. For sure.

Langston spoke into the microphone again. "Now we have a string quartet from Virginia Union College," he said. Langston walked over to a side wall. Four young people walked up to their instruments already set up behind the microphone. They began to play.

"I'm not too crazy about this," Aleesa whispered into Kenneth's ear.

He smiled and shook his head. "Me either," he agreed. "I'd rather hear those guys play the blues. But I'll bet they don't do that during poetry readings. Although I think I read that it's different in the North. The textbook chapter said that in the North, Langston read poetry while guys played the blues in the background."

"Now that would be great!" Aleesa said. "He does use the blues rhythm when he writes sometimes. Just like Radcliffe said. I mean, we even heard it! Like in the banjo dancer poem."

"Shhhhhh!" the woman next to Aleesa whispered with a frown.

Aleesa felt her face get hot. "Sorry!" she answered. She slid down in her chair a little.

The quartet finished playing. They held their instruments and bowed. The audience clapped.

Kenneth and Aleesa looked at each other. Kenneth

shrugged. They clapped too.

"The second part of my program is called 'Negro Dreams,'" Langston announced into the microphone. "These poems will make you think, I hope," he added.

"Just like the man said," Aleesa said in a low voice to Kenneth. "The guy who introduced him." She leaned back in her chair and let the words roll over her.

Kenneth leaned forward. He didn't want to miss a single word. The titles kept coming—"Lenox Avenue: Midnight" and "Harlem Night Club." When Kenneth listened to Langston read "The South," the words seemed to burn his ears.

Was he crazy? Kenneth asked himself. It was almost like a pain in his chest to hear Langston's words. They were true. They were so true, he repeated silently.

"He can really write!" Kenneth exclaimed in a low voice to Aleesa. "That's how I really feel," he added. "Exactly."

The audience was on its feet again. Kenneth and Aleesa joined them, clapping hard. Aleesa kept clapping, even though her hands were stinging.

The noise died down again. Langston stood silently, waiting.

"I always like to end with this," he said. "The title of my last poem is 'I, Too, Sing America.'"

Aleesa listened to the beat of Langston's voice. His words were so strong, she thought. Her nerves almost tingled as he finished.

Kenneth shut his eyes for a second. The force of

Langston's words crowded everything else out of his mind. Words could do so much, he thought. They called up so many feelings. Feelings he hardly knew he had. Langston's voice echoed back and forth in his head.

Langston finished. He looked gravely at the audience. A moment of silence hung in the air. A hush fell over the crowd.

Then, at once, the audience rose to its feet, clapping and cheering.

"That gave me chills!" Aleesa said to Kenneth as they stood clapping loudly. Her eyes were bright. "Why didn't I know about Langston?"

"Because you didn't do your homework, cabbage brain," Kenneth joked.

Kenneth and Aleesa watched while Langston signed poetry books. He chatted with people. He shook hands.

"He's always smiling," Aleesa said in a low voice to Kenneth.

"He knows who he is too," Kenneth said. "He's not afraid to be himself." He watched Langston clap an older man on the shoulder. They laughed together.

After the last members of the audience drifted out, it was late. Kenneth and Aleesa helped pack up the rest of the books. They carried the boxes out to the old Ford.

"Where are the Bluesmen?" Langston asked Radcliffe. He looked around the dark street. "I thought they said they were going to come with us."

Langston smiled at Kenneth and Aleesa. "It looks like we're going to have quite a group traveling together.

There's a Detroit blues band that's asked to follow us for a while."

"They told me they'd meet us at Virginia State College tomorrow," Radcliffe answered.

"What? That blues band is coming along too?" Kenneth asked. They seemed okay, but that Chauncey was a little on the crazy side. His temper could get them all into trouble.

"The blues band is coming with us?" Aleesa asked. She grinned. "The Bluesmen, they're called? That's great!" Those guys would be fun to listen to.

"Just for a while," Langston said. "Maybe they can get more people to come and listen to me. Publicity, you know? They can play in cafes before or after some of my programs. We thought it'd be a good arrangement. They can help sell books for me. I can bring in listeners for them. We're going to have ourselves a regular cultural event here," Langston said.

"Let's get going," Radcliffe said. "Kenneth, you can bunk in our room. Aleesa, our hostess for tonight says she has an extra room. We'll leave early tomorrow morning for Ettrick and Virginia State."

Radcliffe turned the key in the ignition. Everyone else got in. The four doors slammed.

Aleesa swallowed hard. She looked over at Kenneth. Boxes of books were piled high between them. Kenneth raised his eyebrows at Aleesa. He shrugged.

"Here we go," Aleesa whispered. "Like it or not." Her pulse beat faster. What was going to happen to them?

5

Reach Their Hearts

Friday had passed in a blur, Kenneth thought staring out the car window. It was already Saturday morning.

Kenneth turned around. He could see the Bluesmen following in their car. He raised a hand in a wave. Ralph waved back from the front seat.

Kenneth thought back to yesterday. They had all gotten to Virginia State College Friday afternoon. The

Bluesmen had played a few numbers at the auditorium. He and Aleesa had unpacked the boxes of poetry books, *The Weary Blues* and *The Negro Mother.* They'd helped Langston set up.

Then Langston had read his poetry. Everyone had clapped and cheered. Kenneth was proud to be helping. He straightened his shoulders a little.

So far, the Bluesmen hadn't caused any problems— even Chauncey. He had muttered something about how Detroit wasn't like the South. But nothing had happened—yet. They'd all stayed last night with their hosts, another local African American family. A professor at Virginia State College had set it up for them.

Kenneth frowned. Langston told them that most of the colleges on the tour had set up families for them to stay with. African Americans weren't welcome at hotels or motels. And a lot of the towns were small. They had no hotels at all.

Kenneth sighed. He still couldn't believe all of this. Things in the South in 1931 were really bad for African Americans. He had to remember not to use the term "African American" too. No one in 1931 had even heard that term. He shook his head.

In the other corner of the back seat, Aleesa watched the small farms streak by the window. All her worries had been for nothing, she told herself. So far, anyway. She frowned. Except for the signs everywhere reading "colored" and "whites only." She held back a shudder.

That part was a nightmare. Aleesa couldn't imagine how Langston and Radcliffe stood it. Thank goodness Dr. King and the Civil Rights Movement had come along.

But Langston and Radcliffe didn't know anything about Civil Rights, of course. She had to be sure she kept her mouth shut. Aleesa squeezed her eyes shut. What if she and Kenneth couldn't get back home? They'd be doomed to grow up in the Jim Crow South. A chill ran down her spine. She couldn't imagine how that would be.

"Here we are," Radcliffe announced. They slowed to a stop. "Hampton, Virginia," he added. "Hampton Institute."

Aleesa and Kenneth stared at the buildings. Trees clustered around the buildings. It looked nice, Kenneth thought. He wouldn't mind going to college here. Whoa! he remembered. What would Hampton Institute be like in his time—in the future? he wondered. Would it still be here?

"The alma mater of Booker T. Washington," Langston added. "This is where he went to college. I was here last March," he said. "We're reading at Ogden Hall tonight."

"Then after that we'll hear the Bluesmen," Radcliffe added. "They got a last minute gig at a cafe in the Negro section of town," he added.

"Great!" Aleesa said. She smiled. At least she was getting to hear some good music. And Langston's poetry was good. She almost hated to admit that she really liked it. It wasn't like any poetry she'd ever heard before.

Radcliffe drove them to meet their host family. They ate dinner. Then they all piled back into the Ford to go to the college. The Bluesmen followed in their car. The two cars pulled up behind Ogden Hall.

Kenneth and Aleesa helped carry the boxes of poetry books. Langston and Radcliffe set up the tables. The Bluesmen helped with chairs and the microphone.

For a few minutes, Aleesa and Kenneth stood alone next to the entrance.

"Listen," Aleesa said in a low voice. "You said we needed time to figure out how to get home, right? So? Have you decided anything?" she challenged.

"Uh, no," Kenneth admitted. He sighed. "We have to stay alert," he said. "We'll just have to keep watching. Something will turn up."

"Yeah?" Aleesa put her hands on her hips. "Well, I don't see anything," she said. "Except that you're having too good a time listening to Langston's poetry. And the Bluesmen." She narrowed her eyes. "I don't think you really want to get home."

Kenneth frowned. Part of what Aleesa was saying was right. He was having a good time. But he really did want to get home. They both had to get home. Who knew how long it would be before something bad happened? Chauncey in the Bluesmen was like an accident waiting to happen.

"Where's Langston Hughes?" a girl asked, coming into the hall. A group of students followed her.

"He's right outside," Kenneth said. "The program will start in an hour. Can we help you?" he asked.

The girl looked upset. The other students clustered

around her. "We want him to read some of his poetry tomorrow night," she said. "We're going to have a memorial service for the football coach who was beaten to death. He went to college here. Did you know that? And for Juliette Derricote, the Dean at Fisk. You know about them, right?" she asked.

Aleesa and Kenneth looked at each other. Uh-oh, Kenneth thought. He'd almost forgotten about those people. Danger really did surround them here in the South. A worried frown creased his forehead.

"Sure!" Langston's voice reached them. He was standing at the side door. He joined the group of students. "Count me in," he said. "I'll be glad to do what I can. Let me know what time. I'll even help you plan the service," he added.

The students broke into smiles.

"Thanks!" one said.

"Thank you, Mr. Hughes," said another.

"That's swell, Mr. Hughes," a third added.

"And we'll play something too," Chauncey said, walking up the center aisle. The Bluesmen followed him. "We'll do our best."

"That's wonderful!" the girl said. "This will mean a lot." She looked down at the ground. "We think something should be done. We—we can't stop the hatred. But maybe we can make people remember."

"And think about it," Langston added forcefully. "So that change will come."

Did Langston just glance at Chauncey? Kenneth asked himself. It had looked like it.

"We need to make all people think about what they're doing," Langston went on. "But anger with violence does no good. That just makes everyone get more angry."

A hush fell over the group of students. Kenneth looked out of the corner of his eye at Chauncey. What was Chauncey thinking? Chauncey's face looked stern.

"We need change in America," Langston said to the group. "But I think we need to make change happen with our talent. We need to channel our anger and use our gifts. Then we can make them see our Negro people in a different way. We'll tell the truth. But I believe we must tell the truth in a way that others will listen. That's what I try to do with my poetry."

That was why she liked his poetry, Aleesa thought. What Langston wrote was the truth. He knew how she felt.

"We'll check with the college deans," the girl said. "Then we'll plan the service. Thanks, Mr. Hughes."

The students took seats in the auditorium. Soon, the auditorium filled with hundreds and hundreds of students.

Kenneth looked around in amazement. If he were Langston, he'd be scared to death. But Langston just smiled after his introduction. The program went as it always did. Langston began reading. And the crowd fell under the spell of his words.

Shouts of laughter and sudden, awed silences would greet different poems. Finally, cheering and clapping filled the air at the end. Langston's words had so much power, Kenneth thought.

Dozens of students and teachers crowded around Langston after the program. Kenneth and Aleesa sold the poetry books. The Bluesmen helped out. Ralph made change in the cash box. Chauncey was making jokes with the girls. Paul and Hubert kept the stacks of books in order. Langston was shaking hands. He laughed and talked with everyone.

"They said no!" a girl's voice cut through the air. Kenneth looked over. It was the same girl who had led the group of students earlier.

She stood in front of Langston. Other students gathered around.

Kenneth stood next to Chauncey. "See? See?" Chauncey snapped at Kenneth. "What have I been saying? Things have gotta change." He flexed his fingers. "Too bad I need these for the guitar," he said. "I could do a lot of damage with these."

Kenneth stood still. Chauncey could get them all in a lot of trouble. He sure hoped Langston could control Chauncey. Or they'd all end up somewhere they didn't want to be. It was too dangerous.

"I can't believe it!" the girl was saying. Murmurs of protest filled the air. "The dean of men *himself*. He said, 'Here at Hampton, we educate. We don't protest.' And he's one of us too," she almost wailed. "No memorial service!"

Langston shook his head. He paused. "There is fear

everywhere." The group around him fell silent. "And cowardice. In our own people, too, sometimes. I can understand it. They have their reasons," he added. "But we have to change people's minds and hearts. And to reach their hearts, we need poetry." He looked over at Chauncey and the Bluesmen. "And music," he said.

"Right," Chauncey muttered under his breath. Aleesa looked over at Chauncey. He was sure aching for a fight, she thought. She couldn't blame him either. She'd like some of these people to know what it felt like. For sure. She sighed.

"I am sorry about the memorial service," Langston went on. "But you can be sure the world will hear about this. I will write a poem. And I'll tell everyone."

The students began clapping again. Langston held up his hands. "No, no," he said. "I do only what I believe to be right. We'll have freedom. Some day."

That almost sounded like Dr. King's speech, Aleesa thought. She squeezed her eyes shut. If only Langston and Radcliffe and the Bluesmen knew about Dr. King. They would be so happy. But she couldn't say anything. Not a thing. This traveling back in time was rough. She bit her lip. She really wanted to get home. And fast.

The crowd finally left. The Bluesmen drove to the cafe to set up. Radcliffe drove Aleesa, Kenneth, and Langston to the cafe.

If Grandma only knew what she was doing. Going out to a blues cafe at midnight. She giggled to herself in the back seat. This sure beat going to school.

"Our next big stop is the University of North Carolina," Langston said. He turned to look at Kenneth and Aleesa. He stopped for a second. He cleared his throat. "This is—ah—the only white university we've got a firm contract for. It will be interesting," he said. Then he turned to face the front.

Kenneth and Aleesa stared at each other.

"A white college?" Aleesa whispered. Her mouth felt dry. "I don't think that's such a great idea!"

"Me either," Kenneth agreed. He clenched his fists at his side.

And what would Chauncey do?

6
Challenge

"I'm thirsty," Langston announced an hour later.

"Me too," Aleesa said. It was dusty and hot, even for November. Wasn't Berkeley cooler this time of year? Berkeley, she sighed. She twisted her hands together. Would she ever get home again?

Aleesa looked up into the sky. Was there a magic time capsule that would scoop them up? Would it take

51

them back home? She snorted in disgust. She was wacko, for sure.

Kenneth looked at the little store and gas station they pulled up to. He didn't even recognize the brand of gas.

Radcliffe turned off the engine. They stepped out onto the little dusty parking lot. Behind them, the tires of the Bluesmen's car crunched on the gravel.

The little store needed paint. "Eats and Worms" read a faded sign.

"We're thirsty. We're going to get some soda pop," Langston called to them. He began to open the door to the store.

Kenneth watched Langston tug at it. The door didn't budge. Someone was holding it shut!

"You can't come in here," a voice inside snapped at Langston. "Didn't you see the sign? This door is for whites only."

Aleesa shut her eyes for an instant. She couldn't believe this. This was just like those awful movies they saw sometimes. She shuddered. How shameful. How shameful, she repeated silently. Then anger began to bubble up inside her. She clenched her fists at her sides.

Kenneth stood stock still. The man's words echoed in his brain. "For whites only. For whites only." What would Langston do? Behind him, he heard the Bluesmen walk up.

"What is this?" Chauncey's voice hissed. Chauncey came and stood next to Kenneth. Kenneth could almost feel the heat of Chauncey's anger.

"Let's just watch," Kenneth warned him. "Don't say anything." He didn't want Chauncey to do anything stupid. "Let Langston handle it," he added.

Langston was speaking to the man inside. "Well, where's the—ah—colored entrance?" he asked. "I want to buy some soda pop."

"There ain't no colored entrance," the voice sneered. "You have to buy your soda pop through the hole."

"Through the hole?" Langston asked. He turned to face his friends. His face looked puzzled, Aleesa thought. "Through the *hole?*" he repeated.

"Walk around to the side," the voice barked.

Langston shrugged. He walked around to the side of the little store. Aleesa, Kenneth, and the Bluesmen followed.

Kenneth's jaw dropped. The man inside wasn't kidding.

"Would you look at that?" Kenneth asked Aleesa. He pointed at the side of the store. "There is a hole. It's cut right into the side of the store!"

"That's disgusting!" Aleesa proclaimed. "That is just disgusting. We would *never*—unh!" Kenneth grabbed her arm.

"Shhhh!" Kenneth whispered. "You don't know anything different, right? You don't know anything except what you see right here. Or we're in trouble."

Aleesa angrily jerked her arm away. "Don't you be telling me what to do," she snapped. She rubbed her arm. Kenneth! she scoffed silently. He always had to be so right.

Langston stood in front of the square hole cut into the side of the store. He stared at it.

"Well? Whaddaya want?" the voice barked.

Langston began to laugh. "Ha, ha, ha, ha!" He laughed in gulps and gasps.

Kenneth stared in astonishment. Langston thought it was funny. Tears of laughter ran down Langston's cheeks.

"Ha, ha, ha, ha!" Langston slapped his knee. "Isn't that the funniest thing you've ever seen?" he managed to ask. He kept laughing. "Buy your soda through a hole in the wall?" He leaned weakly against the side of the store. "Oh, me. Oh, my," he said.

By then, everyone else had begun to smile. Aleesa felt a smile tugging at the corners of her mouth. Kenneth grinned.

Radcliffe joined in Langston's laughter. Ralph, Hubert, and Paul began to chuckle. Only Chauncey, standing next to Kenneth, snorted silently.

Langston's laughter began to die down. "Oh, me," he repeated. He wiped his eyes, still grinning. He looked at everyone standing there. "Well, I'm not as thirsty as I thought," he said. He shook his head in amazement. "Doesn't that beat the band?" he asked. "A hole in the wall!"

Everyone walked back to the two cars parked in the dusty little lot. Kenneth noticed Chauncey kicking little bits of gravel. They skittered in front of his shoes.

"I don't think it's so funny," Chauncey said to Langston. "I'd like to take that guy and show him a thing

or two. I don't think it's funny at all. I think it's—it's—"
He stopped, at a loss for the right word.

"It's the way it is right now," Langston said smoothly.
He stopped and looked at Chauncey evenly. "Now, look
here," Langston said. He stared up at Chauncey. "I know
things are wrong here in the South. They're wrong in a lot
of the North too. But that doesn't mean we do the same
things they do. We won't sink to their level."

That was a good way to say it, Kenneth thought. He
glanced at Aleesa. He hoped she was listening.

Aleesa caught Kenneth's glance. She made a face at
him. He always thought he was right. What a jerk. Yeah,
yeah, yeah. She guessed Langston had some good ideas.
But she was still mad.

Langston was still talking to Chauncey. "You hear
what my poetry says. Send the people a message,
Chauncey. You're a musician. Write the songs. Play the
blues. Send the message."

Then Langston turned and got into the old Ford.
Kenneth watched while Chauncey stalked back to the
Bluesmen's car. His face still looked angry.

The car doors slammed. Radcliffe started the engine.
The car pulled out of the lot. Dust billowed up in the air.
The Bluesmen's car followed them, crunching onto the
main road.

"Whew!" Langston exclaimed. He rolled up his
window quickly. "There's a lot of dirt out here." Then he
looked at Kenneth and Aleesa. "A *lot* of dirt, right?" he

joked. He jerked his head in the direction of the store and its owner. "Dirt, for sure."

"Yeah," Aleesa said slowly. She leaned her head back against the seat. The way Langston handled things was amazing. She had a lot to think about.

"Dirt is right," Kenneth said. He smiled, shaking his head at the same time. He settled back and watched the scenery.

Then Kenneth remembered something. They were on their way to a white university. Look what had happened just trying to buy a can of soda. What was going to happen at the University of North Carolina?

"Uh, Langston?" Kenneth began. "When are we getting to the University of North Carolina?" he asked. He hoped it wouldn't be too soon. He wasn't ready for it yet. He might not ever be ready for it.

Langston reached into the glove box. He looked at a calendar. "Not for another—ah—twelve days," Langston said. "We've got plenty of schools, halls, and churches before then." He put the calendar back. "We'll play at the Full Gospel Church tonight in the next town. The Bluesmen have a place to play too. We'll be in Chapel Hill at the University of North Carolina on November nineteenth."

Kenneth and Aleesa exchanged glances. Would they have to go to Chapel Hill too? Kenneth wondered. Or would they be back home by then? How were they going to find a way home?

He kept looking at everything they passed. He didn't even know what he was looking for. Something— something that looked familiar maybe? But nothing looked promising. Nothing looked like Berkeley. And no one had come up to them and asked them if they wanted a ride ahead to their own time. He sighed.

On her side of the back seat, Aleesa sighed. She definitely did not want to go to an all-white university. After what just happened at the little store? Nuh-uh. Would they find a way to get home before then? she wondered.

A few hours later, Radcliffe called out, "There it is!"

Kenneth's eyes popped open. He must have dozed off. Dang. Did he miss anything? A way to get home?

The two cars pulled up next to a small cafe. "The Hot Spot" read the sign in blue letters.

"What's this?" Aleesa asked. She peered out the window.

"This is where Chauncey and the guys are playing," Langston said. He turned around to face Kenneth and Aleesa. "We'll drop off their instruments. They can set up. Then we'll go meet our host families. We don't have to be at the Full Gospel Church until seven-thirty. The program starts at eight."

The Bluesmen were already unpacking their instruments. Chauncey had the trunk of the old car open. The others began carrying instruments and cases across the dusty sidewalk. Ralph held the door of the cafe open.

Kenneth and Aleesa hopped out of the car. Langston and Radcliffe rolled down the windows.

"Can we help?" Kenneth asked. He grabbed a music stand from Hubert.

"Hey!" a rude voice exclaimed. "You're in our way!"

Kenneth whipped around. Two white boys about his age stood in the center of the sidewalk. They had their thumbs hooked in their pockets. Their eyes were narrowed.

"What are ya? Deaf as well as dumb?" the bigger boy scoffed.

He elbowed the smaller boy. The smaller boy snickered.

"I said, you're in our way!" the big one repeated. He spit on the ground.

Kenneth stood stock still. Was this really happening to him? He'd like to just deck 'em. But—this was the South. This was the South in 1931. Who knew what would happen to him if he decked the guy? No. He knew what might happen.

He could get killed for it.

7

Trouble Ahead?

Kenneth swallowed hard. He took a deep breath. His heart pounded, but he lifted his chin.

"Look," he began. His voice shook a little. "I don't know—"

"You two!" Chauncey's voice broke in. He glared at the two white boys. Then he stepped next to Kenneth. Menace hung in the air between his words. His fists were clenched.

Aleesa held her breath. This was going to be ugly. She wanted to shut her eyes. Was this going to be the end? Oh, why couldn't they be back in Berkeley?

A car door slammed. Langston jumped out of the Ford. He moved between Chauncey and Kenneth and the two boys.

Kenneth could almost hear his heart beat in the sudden silence. What would happen now? Did he read about this in the social studies book? Did Langston get beat up by people in the South? Why couldn't he remember?

Langston looked at the two boys. "Let me handle this," he said. He didn't give them a chance to answer. The two boys scowled, but they stepped back. Langston turned to Kenneth and Chauncey.

"Look," Langston said in an even voice. "Anyone can hit. It takes no brains to be violent. Or to just be quiet and not try to change things. You know that." He stared at Chauncey. "You've got brains. You have a gift. Your music is a gift. Use it for good. Use it to say how you feel. Speak to our people. Speak to the others."

Aleesa saw Chauncey relax his fists. He took a deep breath. But he was still frowning.

"Use your gift," Langston went on. "That's something different. That's what people will pay attention to. Not the same old anger. Not the same old put up and shut up either. Not like the dean at Hampton Institute," he added. "The one who said 'we don't protest.' Where do those ways of thinking get you?" he asked. "*You* think about it too," he told Kenneth.

Kenneth looked down at the ground. Frustration bubbled up inside him. There was so much he wanted to say to Langston. How in his time the Jim Crow laws were gone. He wanted to tell Langston about Civil Rights. And how African Americans didn't have to put up with being treated like that anymore. And how things were changing for the better. He clenched his fists. But he had to stay quiet. It was hard.

Langston turned to the two white boys. He looked at them evenly. "Now if you don't mind," he said with dignity, "we'll finish up here and get out of your way." He reached down and picked up a guitar case. He walked into the cafe without a backward look.

Aleesa watched the two boys. They kept their thumbs hooked in their pockets. They frowned. They looked as if they were pretending to be tough. Huh, she thought. They knew they'd be no match against seven people—not even counting her. And she was probably the meanest, she snickered silently.

Working quickly, everyone hauled the last instruments inside the little cafe. The cafe owner shut the door behind them. They all stared at each other for a moment.

Inside the small cafe, Aleesa sank down on a rickety chair. She was shaking. That could have turned out really ugly.

Snap! Snap! Snap! Chauncey opened his guitar case. He lifted out his guitar. He ran a hard riff down the scale.

Aleesa could tell he was still really mad.

One of the boys' jeering voices from outside broke the silence. "Watch out!" he called. "You better watch yourselves. Remember what's happening to the Scottsboro Boys!"

Kenneth froze. He remembered *that* from the textbook. That was horrible. He'd forgotten the *Scottsboro* case was in 1931. He shuddered. He lifted the curtain at a window. The boys were strutting down the street. Soon they'd be gone. Whew, he thought.

"Who are the Scottsboro Boys?" Aleesa asked. She looked at Kenneth. "It doesn't sound too good. I don't remember that! Did you read—?"

"The *Scottsboro Boys* case. Another example of ugliness, injustice, and hatred," Langston broke in, frowning.

Kenneth's stomach tightened. Aleesa better not say anything more. What if she said something about the textbook right in front of everyone? Good thing Langston had interrupted her. Kenneth's forehead beaded up with cold sweat. That would have been hard to explain.

"I'm writing a poem about the *Scottsboro* case right now," Langston went on. "Two young, white magazine editors from Chapel Hill, where the University of North Carolina is, asked me to write it. They'll publish it when we get there. And I'll let people know what I think about the Scottsboro Boys in the poem. It's called 'Christ in Alabama.' I promise you it'll make people think hard."

"Will the poem be published when we get to Chapel Hill?" Kenneth asked. He swallowed hard.

"Yes, it will," answered Langston.

"Won't that be kind of dangerous?" Kenneth asked.

"It could be," Langston admitted. "Words are dangerous. They have power. They have the power to move. They also have the power to change. We all have to make changes." He sat down on a chair next to Aleesa. "We have to reach our own people too," he said.

Langston looked at the Bluesmen and Kenneth. They had formed a small semicircle around Langston and Aleesa.

"No writer or musician has really said what it's like to be a Negro," Langston said. "No one speaks or sings or plays as a Negro. Too many of us writers have been too busy trying to please white people.

"Think about how we couldn't have the memorial service for the football coach in Virginia. Too many Negro writers are trying to please just the educated Negroes. Even some of the other Harlem poets and writers.

"But not me. Everyone said I couldn't turn poetry into bread. They said I couldn't make a living doing this."

Langston grinned and leaned back in the chair. He shook his head.

"I've gotten lots of Negroes mad at me too," he said with a chuckle. "For what I write about."

Langston stood up for a second and reached into his pocket. He pulled out a letter. Unfolding it, he sat down again.

"Listen to this. My friend Carl in New York just sent this on to me. It came addressed to me at his office." Langston cleared his throat. "Dear Mr. Hughes," he read.

He looked up. Aleesa saw everyone was listening. Even Chauncey.

"I am disgusted by your poems," Langston read. "As a fellow Negro, I don't think you should write like that. People don't want to read about Harlem. They don't want to read about jazz clubs and the low life. They need to be inspired and encouraged. They don't need to read this kind of trash."

Silence followed. Then Langston threw his head back and laughed. Aleesa and Kenneth looked at each other. They began to smile. Langston's laughter sure was catching.

"Oh, me," he gasped when he had a chance to draw a breath. "Who do these people think they are, anyway? Just because I write poetry for the common man, not only the educated Negroes."

Langston laughed again. He folded the letter up. Standing up, he slipped the envelope into his pocket.

Then he looked at everyone. "You've seen for yourselves. You see how many people come to hear the program, right? The common man wants and needs poetry too." He chuckled. "You know how it is. They want poetry. I must have shaken hundreds of hands on this tour already. I've signed autographs on the funniest things—napkins and scraps of paper."

Langston's face sobered. "Poets—and musicians—need to give a voice to the common man. We need to show how everyone feels. And we need to see the value of being ourselves—whoever we are."

That was another reason she liked his poetry, Aleesa realized. Langston's poetry made her feel good to be herself. How did he do that?

No wonder Langston Hughes was famous, Kenneth thought. No wonder so many people came to the poetry readings and got so excited.

"Well, we'd better go meet our host families," Langston said. He stood up. The Bluesmen finished setting up their instruments. The cafe owner said good-bye.

Out in the dusty street, Aleesa watched the Bluesmen get into their car. Chauncey slammed the door hard. She and Kenneth exchanged glances.

"Looks like Chauncey still has a few problems," Kenneth commented. Radcliffe started up the car.

Langston looked over the back of the front seat. "Yeah," he agreed. "I keep hoping he'll see the light. But he has a lot of anger in him still." Langston shook his head. He turned back to face the front.

Langston was right, Kenneth told himself. Chauncey could get them all in trouble. Or worse. And Chapel Hill was coming closer too. What would Chauncey do in an all-white university town?

"Are—are you sure it's a good idea to publish the Scottsboro poem in Chapel Hill?" Kenneth asked. He didn't want to sound like a wimp. He wasn't a wimp on the football field. Or anywhere. But he wanted to get home to Berkeley. He didn't want to die in the South.

Langston turned around again. "It's always a good idea to tell the truth about evil. To make people think. And if my poems do that, that's all I want. Then change will come." He smiled and turned back to face the front.

Langston was brave, Aleesa thought. Her heart lifted a little. This poetry stuff was all right. And things had started changing too—ahead in her time. Langston really thought about stuff. He had a vision. Just like Dr. King had said. Grandma always talked about that. If only she and Kenneth could share that with Langston—and the Bluesmen too.

Later that night before the program, people packed into the Full Gospel Church. There weren't enough chairs for people, Kenneth realized. Dozens of people crowded in the narthex. So many people wanted to hear Langston.

Langston's voice hypnotized the audience. Kenneth watched their faces. Laughter, joy, sadness, anger, understanding, compassion, fear, and hope visited each face in turn. At the end of the program, Langston finished with "I, Too, Sing America." People cheered and clapped. They stomped their feet.

"The crowd's going crazy," Aleesa said to Kenneth over the noise of the crowd. "They sure like what Langston reads." She leaned forward to watch everyone.

"Uh-huh. It's just like he said," Kenneth agreed. He talked loudly into her ear. "Poetry can mean something to everyone. It's not only for the educated. It's for all people. And that's the way to spread the word. That's how things change. People have to think about what they're doing."

"Yeah," Aleesa said. She glanced over at the Bluesmen on the other side of the crowded church. "But tell that to Chauncey. He's still not agreeing with Langston. I can tell he's still angry."

"You're right. He's still ready to punch someone out," Kenneth said. "We'll just have to watch him. Especially when we get to Chapel Hill." He frowned. "That could be ugly."

"Maybe we can find a way to get home first," Aleesa said. She looked hopefully at Kenneth. "Then we wouldn't have to worry about it," she added. Her face twisted with worry. "I don't want to die—or get beaten up—or anything," she said.

Kenneth tightened his mouth. He frowned. "I don't know what we're going to do," he said. "Maybe when we get to Chapel Hill we can visit their library. After all, that's how we ended up here, right? It was a university library. Maybe that'll work somehow."

Aleesa winced. "It'd be a lot better if we could go home *before* Chapel Hill," she said.

Kenneth sighed. "I wish I could remember what happened in history," he said in a low voice. "But I really don't think this college tour of Langston's is in our textbook at all."

"You mean, no one knows about this poetry program tour?" Aleesa almost squeaked. "They won't know what Langston was trying to do? About bringing his poetry to the people?"

"I'm sure some people do," Kenneth scoffed. "All they have to do is read a book about Langston Hughes's life. But no, students won't usually know. Unless someone tells them."

Aleesa was silent for a minute. All around them, people crowded up to the front. Langston was shaking hands. He was laughing. He signed dozens of autographs.

"Well, if we get back," Aleesa said. She swallowed hard. "If we get back, we can do something about this for our project, right?"

"Yeah," Kenneth said. "But we'll have to be careful. We can't let anyone know we time-traveled." He laughed. "I mean, really. Who'd believe us? They'd take us to the loony bin."

"You're right," Aleesa said. She sighed. "I just want to get home. I miss Berkeley. I miss Grandma. Even being grounded." A smile began to creep across her face. "I *almost* miss social studies." She looked at Kenneth. Her smile faded. "Can't you figure out a way for us to get home? Before we have to go to the University of North Carolina?" she begged.

8
A Trap?

A week later, Aleesa and Kenneth carried boxes of books into a meeting hall.

"We've sure sold a lot of these. I'm glad Langston's publisher friend in New York keeps sending us more books." Kenneth wiped his forehead with his sleeve.

"I can't believe how much of Langston's stuff we're selling," Aleesa agreed. She began pulling books out of the boxes. She stacked them on the table. She reached in for pamphlets. Langston had lots of his poems printed up to sell in pamphlets, not only books. And people were buying them as fast as they could.

Kenneth looked at the display they were setting up. "I like how he wants everyone to know about other African American writers too," he added. "Look at all these other books we've carried around. Lots of people are getting excited about what African Americans are doing. It's making them proud."

Aleesa looked around. "You'd better be careful." She smirked. "You don't want anyone to hear you saying 'African American.' Hah!" she said triumphantly. Kenneth didn't do *everything* right.

After the program a few hours later, Kenneth and Aleesa packed boxes up again. A few people were still standing in line to meet Langston. He was signing the last autographs.

"Things are going okay, huh?" Aleesa asked. "I mean, we're getting this down, right?" She thumped more books down inside the box. "Except for getting home, I mean," she said. She made a face.

Kenneth looked at her. He held a stack of books. "Okay?" he repeated. "Did you forget where we'll be in four days? Chapel Hill?" he asked. "And how Chauncey keeps getting really mad at all the Jim Crow junk? Like colored drinking fountains. He says that they don't look colored to him."

Kenneth sighed. He shook his head. "It's a good thing the Bluesmen are busy. They've been playing a lot of blues in little cafes and stuff. It keeps Chauncey out of trouble."

Aleesa bit her lip. "No, I didn't forget. I guess I just don't want to think about it," she said.

"You didn't forget what?" Langston asked. He and Radcliffe began folding up the table.

"Uh, about Chapel Hill. The University of North Carolina. And your poem about the Scottsboro Boys," Aleesa said. "It's an all-white school, right?"

Langston smiled. "I don't think that's changed," he said. He reached for another table leg. "But a few days ago, I got another letter from those two young white men—the editors of the magazine *Contempo*. Anthony Buttitta and Milton Abernethy. They've invited us to stay with them. Can you imagine that?"

No, he couldn't, Kenneth told himself. Those guys had to be crazy to do that in this time.

"That's brave," Langston went on. "They're inviting Negroes to stay with them. No other white person has done that on this trip. Remember how they wanted me to write a poem about the *Scottsboro* case? Now they want me to write an article about the case too. I wrote it and mailed it already."

Langston snapped the last leg of the table into place. He stood up.

"They'll publish that in *Contempo* along with the poem. People won't believe what I wrote! It's—well—I guess you'd say it's sarcastic and teasing." Langston grinned. "Kind of like other things I write. Pretty good, eh? I'll get lots of publicity. I'll get a crowd at the poetry reading."

That's not all you'll get, Kenneth wanted to say. But Langston sure was brave. Nothing seemed to bother him. Kenneth shook his head.

"You're not worried?" Kenneth asked.

"Like I always say. If people don't face the evil around them, they won't change." Langston smiled. "Wait until people read the article I wrote," he laughed. "It's a good one. It'll get their attention, all right."

"You've got guts," Radcliffe said over his shoulder. He carried the table over to the wall.

Kenneth repeated Radcliffe's words the next morning. "You've got guts," Radcliffe had told Langston. Kenneth stared out the car window. The scenery whisked by. But did *he* have guts?

Kenneth looked over his shoulder at the Bluesmen following in their car. Chauncey still had a problem. Every time something bad happened, anger burned in his eyes. Kenneth shivered a little.

"Let's stop. I want to get a newspaper," Langston said in the front seat. "The book review section of the *New York Times*. I want to find out what's happening in the book world. I haven't seen it for a while."

They drove into the next town. "Probably at the train station," Langston said. "That's the only place that might have the *New York Times* in this town." He laughed.

Radcliffe found the train station. They pulled up in the parking lot. The Bluesmen drove in after them.

Langston stepped out of the car. He walked toward the little railroad station. Aleesa watched him open the door. He vanished inside. Book review section, she thought. That's pretty brainy stuff. It sure wasn't anything *she'd* pick out of the newspaper to read.

"Langston's won quite a few writing awards, you know," Radcliffe said from the front seat. "He's famous in the New York literary world. Lots of authors and poets are proud to call him a friend. White and Negro both."

The minutes passed. Radcliffe, Kenneth, and Aleesa talked about some of Langston's poems. Aleesa kept watching the door of the railroad station. Langston still didn't come out.

"And so that's when Langston wrote 'The Negro Speaks of Rivers,' " Radcliffe was saying.

Chauncey knocked on Kenneth's window. Kenneth rolled it down.

"What's going on?" Chauncey asked. "Langston's been in there a long time. He hasn't come out." Chauncey's face darkened. "Do you think he's okay?"

Kenneth and Radcliffe got out of the car. Aleesa rolled down her window. Something definitely wasn't right. She wiped her clammy hands on her dress. Something must have happened to Langston.

"I don't hear anything," Radcliffe said, puzzled. Now

the other Bluesmen got out of the car.

"Hey, what's going on?" Ralph asked.

"Is Langston all right?" Hubert asked.

Chauncey set his jaw. He put his shoulders back.

"You guys can all stand here," Chauncey said. "I'm not. I'm going in there. It doesn't say 'whites only' on the door. For once," he snorted.

Kenneth and Aleesa looked at each other. Uh-oh, Aleesa mouthed to Kenneth.

What could he do now? Kenneth asked himself. He was in pretty good shape from football. But Chauncey was a lot older and bigger.

"Uh—" Kenneth began. He took a step toward Chauncey.

"Hey!" Hubert called. He pointed down the tracks. "There he is!"

Sure enough, Langston's slight figure appeared. Aleesa's jaw dropped. Langston was walking along the railroad tracks!

"How did he get out there?" Kenneth exclaimed. "What is he doing, anyway?"

"I didn't see him come out of the railroad station waiting room, did you?" Aleesa asked. Langston waved to them. He smiled and shook his head.

"What happened?" Radcliffe called out. "And where's your *New York Times?*"

"You're probably wondering why I walked along the railroad tracks," Langston said, joining them. He sighed.

"You won't believe this one." He laughed a short burst of laughter.

"I went in and bought a *New York Times*. A policeman was standing in the waiting room. After I bought the newspaper, I turned to go out the door."

Langston looked back at the railroad station house. Then he looked back at everyone.

"The policeman stopped me. 'Negroes can't use that door,' he said. 'That's only for whites.' 'But I just came in that way,' I told him. I looked around for another door. There was no other door!" Langston laughed a short laugh again.

Kenneth stared. This was unbelievable.

"What did you do?" Chauncey broke in. He doubled up his fists. "I would have just pushed my way through." He scowled.

Kenneth watched Chauncey. Good thing Chauncey hadn't gone in after Langston. That could have been bad.

"So, I asked him a question. How was I going to get out of the waiting room?" Langston went on. He had a half-grin on his face. "Or was I going to have to spend the rest of my life there?" Langston began laughing. "It was getting ridiculous. I could come in. But I couldn't go out the same way!"

Aleesa began to giggle. Kenneth laughed. Radcliffe joined in. The Bluesmen did too—except for Chauncey, Kenneth noticed. He held back a sigh.

"That's when the stationmaster showed me,"

Langston continued. "You're not going to believe this." His grin grew wider. "There was a chute leading to the railroad tracks. That's where they loaded luggage. *That* was my exit. The policeman told me I had to walk along the tracks to get out."

Langston raised one eyebrow. He turned and looked back at the tracks. "So I left the newspaper there. Forget it, I told myself. And *that's* how I got out."

Langston looked around at everyone's faces. "If those people only knew how stupid they looked!" He snorted with laughter. "I got in! But I couldn't get out! I could have grown to be an old man in there!" Langston pulled at an imaginary beard. He pretended to bend over and walk with a cane.

Everyone laughed. But Kenneth watched Chauncey. Chauncey only frowned.

Finally, the laughter died down. Chauncey looked at everyone. "I just thought of something," Chauncey said. "These Jim Crow laws are bad. And we're going to an all-white university. And those two white guys—Buttitta and Abernethy—want you to write an article besides your poem. And now they want us to stay with them." Chauncey's frown deepened. "Hasn't anyone thought of something?" he asked.

"What?" Langston asked. He wiped the tears of laughter from his eyes.

Aleesa watched Chauncey. He was going to say something scary, she could tell. She squeezed her hands together. Was he going to threaten people? Who knew?

"Haven't you wondered if Buttitta and Abernethy are setting us up?" Chauncey asked in a low voice.

A silence fell. Kenneth and Aleesa stared at each other. Kenneth glanced at Langston. He looked surprised.

"What do you mean?" Langston asked. He tilted his head sideways and looked at Chauncey.

"I mean—it looks suspicious to me," Chauncey answered. "Think about it. Two white guys. They ask you to write a poem about the Scottsboro Boys. Everyone in the U.S. is angry about that case. Then they ask you to write an article about it too.

"On top of that—" Chauncey stopped for a gulp of air. He gestured with his arms. "On top of that, they invite us to *stay* with them. The first white people in the South to do that. Hah!" Chauncey exploded. He smacked a fist into his open hand. "They've got something planned for us. Something bad."

He looked at everyone's face. Aleesa felt goose bumps rise on her arms. What if Chauncey was right?

9
Kicked Out!

Kenneth's jaw dropped. Could Chauncey be right?
After all, it did sound strange. Maybe they *were* being set
up. An icy chill feathered down his spine.

Aleesa felt her heart beat faster. What if they were
walking into a trap? She'd never get home again! Why,
oh, why, had she agreed to come? She squeezed her eyes
shut for a second.

Langston stood still. He looked at Chauncey. He took a deep breath. Then he exhaled.

"You know, Chauncey," he began. "Things are bad here in the South. We know that. Jim Crow laws and all that. But that doesn't mean that everyone feels that way. Remember, one of the reasons I can even make this tour is because of some white people."

Langston began to pace up and down. He clasped his hands behind his back.

"One of them is my friend Carl Van Vechten in New York. And my other partner, Prentiss Taylor, is white too. And white professors from the University of North Carolina are the ones who invited me to read there. They are writers themselves."

Well, that was something anyway, Aleesa thought. Maybe there was a little hope. A little. Maybe they would be all right at the university.

Langston stopped and looked at Chauncey. "You have to have some faith," Langston said. "You're angry. And that anger clouds your judgment."

Kenneth saw that the Bluesmen were all staring at Chauncey. Chauncey set his jaw. He stared down at the ground.

"You don't know," Chauncey muttered. "No one knows." Then he looked back up at Langston. "What about your poem and article? What happens when all the people read those? The ones who *aren't* your friends?"

"We'll handle that when we come to it." Langston

sighed. "You gotta have a little faith, man." Then he smiled. "Let's get going. Faith alone isn't going to get us to Chapel Hill on time."

Everyone piled back into the cars. Engines roared to life. The two cars pulled out of the railroad station lot. "Chapel Hill—60 miles," Kenneth read on the road sign.

"Hey," Aleesa whispered to Kenneth. She glanced at the front seat. Langston and Radcliffe were busy talking. The radio played softly. "Hey, Kenneth," she repeated.

Kenneth turned. "What?" he asked.

"Langston said we had to have faith," Aleesa said. "But faith alone isn't going to do it," Aleesa said in a low voice. She had a sinking feeling in the pit of her stomach.

"Something bad is going to happen in Chapel Hill. I know it." Aleesa's face twisted with worry. "This is the same feeling I get when I know Grandma is going to ground me again. Only worse." Suddenly, unshed tears stung her eyes. Grandma. Would she ever see Grandma again? "Besides, how are we going to get home?" she wailed softly.

In his corner of the back seat, Kenneth looked at Aleesa. He shook his head slowly. "I don't know," he admitted. "But remember. We're going to go to the library at the university. Maybe, just maybe, that'll be the answer. I've been thinking. It's a university library. Maybe that'll help us get back to the university library in Berkeley," he said.

Kenneth hoped he sounded confident. It was a pretty

weak idea, he confessed to himself. They dropped out of sight at one university library. Could they get back in another one? He sighed. Probably not.

"At least Langston knows Chauncey's like a bomb ready to go off," Kenneth went on in a whisper. "I'll watch out for him."

Kenneth went back to staring out the window. He was going to have to be extra alert.

There was something else he didn't want to tell Aleesa. He'd have to watch her too. Who knew what she would say? Or do? Especially if Chauncey got mad. Aleesa just popped off all the time. Kenneth sighed. He crossed his fingers for luck.

"Chapel Hill, next stop," Radcliffe finally called out. "Hand me Buttitta and Abernethy's address and directions, Langston," he said. "We'll go to their bookshop. That's where they publish *Contempo* too, right?"

"That's what they wrote me," Langston answered.

Radcliffe wheeled the car around the corner. A few miles later, they pulled up in front of a building. The Bluesmen parked behind them.

Aleesa looked at the signs on each window. "Dry Cleaners." "Tobacco Shop." "Campus Books" and "*Contempo* magazine." That was it. She squeezed her hands together. She glanced over at Kenneth. Was he as nervous as she was?

Kenneth saw the sign too. At least there weren't a hundred people outside waiting to jump on them. Maybe the poem and article hadn't been published in *Contempo* yet.

Kenneth and Aleesa slowly followed Langston and Radcliffe. The Bluesmen hung around outside. Langston looked at the Bluesmen.

"Aren't you coming in?" he asked. "I know they'll want to meet you."

Chauncey looked at Ralph, Paul, and Hubert. "We were gonna wait till you came out," Chauncey said. "But I guess we'll go inside. We'll still keep an eye on what's happening outside. We'll make sure things are okay." He scowled. "I still think this is a setup."

Hubert and Paul nodded in agreement.

"Yeah," Ralph said. "Let's go inside. We'll see what these guys are really up to."

Inside the tiny bookstore, two young white men looked up from their work. They both smiled.

"You must be Langston Hughes!" one of them said with a grin. "I recognize you from your picture in the *New York Times!*" He looked at everyone. "And these must be your friends—and the Bluesmen."

The man put down the books he was holding. He hurried around the counter. He shook everyone's hand. Aleesa giggled. Kenneth shook his hand, surprised.

"This is an honor, let me tell you," the man said enthusiastically. "I'm Milton Abernethy." He gestured at the other young man who was already shaking Kenneth's hand. "That's Anthony. Anthony Buttitta." Milton paused to take a breath. "This is such an honor! I can't tell you!" he exclaimed.

Aleesa raised her eyebrows at Kenneth. This didn't look like a setup to her.

Kenneth gave her a thumbs-up. Maybe things would be all right. He relaxed a little.

"Your poem 'Christ in Alabama' is amazing!" Anthony said. He pumped Langston's hand up and down. "And so is the article. We're publishing them on the first page of *Contempo!* We're gonna shake up this town! Chapel Hill and the university will never be the same."

"Yup!" Milton agreed. "And they need to be shaken up a bit too." He nodded his head forcefully.

Aleesa and Kenneth exchanged glances again. Uh-oh, Aleesa mouthed to Kenneth. It may not be a setup. But they could get into real trouble. Shake up the town?

Great, Kenneth thought. That's all they needed to happen. Shake up a Southern town with African American poetry. And an article about the *Scottsboro Boys* case. Terrific.

"Actually," Anthony said. He looked sort of sheepish, Aleesa thought. His face turned red. "It already has gotten shaken up." He glanced over at Milton. "I guess we'd better tell them."

"Tell us what?" Aleesa burst out. Everyone turned to look at her.

Langston began laughing. "Calm down, girl," he said. "I can run this show. It's all right."

Anthony sighed. "We—ah—we can't have you all stay with us," he said. "I'm really sorry."

Chauncey was right, Kenneth thought. He shoved his hands in his pockets. This was going to be some kind of a setup. He stepped closer to Langston. He wasn't going to miss a word.

"The truth is," Milton said, "we don't even have a place to stay ourselves." He grimaced. "We got kicked out of our rooming house. Our landlady heard we'd invited Negroes to stay with us. So we had to move out this morning."

Kenneth's mouth dropped open. That wasn't what he'd expected to hear. Not at all.

"I'm sorry to hear that," Langston said. He shook his head. "I'm sorry we're the reason you lost your rooms."

"Typical," Anthony snorted. "Typical small-minded people. We wanted to show everyone that we didn't believe in stupidities like prejudice. But we'll show them tomorrow."

He picked up a magazine off the countertop. Kenneth read *Contempo* in big letters. Anthony held it in the air.

"This will help to bring change," Anthony went on. "Your poem and article are right on the front page. And the magazine goes out tomorrow morning. Then your program is tomorrow night. In Gerrard Hall. It'll be packed!"

"Where will we sleep?" Aleesa asked. She twisted her hands together.

"Don't worry," Anthony said with a smile. "We've already arranged a host family for all of you." He looked out the storefront window. "Including the Bluesmen. They're staying with you too. A Negro businessman's family is very happy to take you all in for your stay."

"Thanks!" Ralph said. "Thanks for taking care of us."

"Uh, yeah, thanks," Chauncey said.

Did he hear a note of surprise in Chauncey's voice? Kenneth asked himself. He glanced at Chauncey's face. Yeah. Chauncey did look surprised. Well, actually, he was kind of surprised himself. This poetry and writer stuff must really bring people together, he guessed.

"What about you two?" Langston asked. "I feel responsible for what happened."

"Nah," Milton said. "That's all right. It's worth it. We're staying with friends." He looked at all of them. "We're glad you're here. The president of the University of North Carolina knows you're coming too. Some people wanted him to cancel your poetry program. But he refused."

"Thank you for finding us a place to stay," Langston said. "I'm sorry we caused you some problems."

"Don't worry," Anthony said. "We're happy to have such a famous poet here. Everyone is excited. We'll arrange for you to visit classes on Friday. And we'll take you all out to dinner." He grinned. "In a white cafeteria. Just let them dare to kick you out. The famous poet Langston Hughes!"

SHATTER WITH WORDS: LANGSTON HUGHES

Kenneth and Aleesa looked at each other again. Aleesa shrugged. Well, maybe these two guys knew what they were doing. In her own time, eating in a restaurant with white people was nothing. No one even thought about it. But in 1931—now—in the South?

Kenneth shook his head. He didn't know about all of this. Too many things were happening. And they were happening too fast.

Kenneth looked down at the issue of *Contempo* on the counter. Sure enough. Huge headlines. "Christ in Alabama" by Langston Hughes, he read. And a drawing too. Langston's article about the *Scottsboro Boys* case was right next to it. He glanced at the whole title. Then he began reading Langston's article. He felt the blood drain from his face as he read the words.

Once *Contempo* magazine hit the streets, they were all going to be in big trouble.

10
Shatter with Words

Kenneth lay awake most of the night. Thoughts raced through his head. Sure, people could get along. He knew that from his own time. And even from watching those two guys last night.

Kenneth punched his pillow into shape. What was it that Langston always said? How he wanted people to think about the evil around them. Then change would come. That's why he wrote what he did. Kenneth rubbed his eyes.

Fine, he sighed. Everyone in Chapel Hill who read Langston's poem and article tomorrow would definitely have to think about the evil around them. And they'd probably come after him, Aleesa, Langston, and everyone. His heart thudded a little faster.

He rolled over and drew up the covers. He'd just have to stay cool. *And* watch Chauncey. Who knew what Chauncey would try if people got angry? Kenneth shivered under the blankets.

Early the next afternoon, Kenneth and Aleesa stood in Gerrard Hall on campus. They were setting up Langston's books. Aleesa was putting some of the African American writers' books on the table.

"Hey!" A voice burst into the stillness of the theater. "Hey, listen!"

Aleesa and Kenneth looked up. Chauncey raced toward them. The Bluesmen followed.

"What's up?" Kenneth asked. But from the look on Chauncey's face, he already knew. He felt his stomach tighten. There was going to be trouble after all.

Aleesa straightened up. Her fingers froze on a pile of books. This was her nightmare coming true. Fear prickled her scalp. She was never going to get home. Never.

"The whole town is going crazy," Chauncey exclaimed. "Everyone's talking about Langston's article. And the poem 'Christ in Alabama.' And some people are begging the president of the university to cancel Langston's program!" Chauncey stopped. He gulped for air.

"At least the president said no again. He said he believes in freedom of speech. But he's called out the police to guard us tonight!" Ralph added.

"I think that's a good idea!" Kenneth said, trying to sound confident.

"But what happens next?" Chauncey demanded. "Huh?" He rolled up his sleeves. "I think it's gonna be time to break some heads. We've gotta be ready. The police can't protect us everywhere."

He began pacing back and forth. The other Bluesmen stood silently. Ralph looked worried, Aleesa thought. She didn't blame him. Chauncey was definitely a loose cannon.

"I'm not just going to stand by and face the music quietly," Chauncey snapped. He shook his fist in the air. "I'm gonna take some of those jerks down with me."

Great, Kenneth thought. He looked at Chauncey's angry face. Wait. What had Chauncey just said? "Face the music?" Wasn't that some old-time expression? But he could figure out what it meant. And that made him think of something.

"Look," Kenneth began. He stopped. He took a deep

breath. "Maybe that's what you need to do," he said. "Face the music." He glanced at Aleesa. She was giving him a thumbs-up sign.

Chauncey stopped his pacing. He stepped closer to Kenneth and Aleesa. "What do you mean? Stand there and take it? Huh-uh. I'm gonna fight back!"

"*No!*" Kenneth exclaimed "Think about it. What has Langston been saying this whole time? What has everyone so worked up?" Kenneth asked.

Kenneth paused. He looked searchingly into Chauncey's face. He took a deep breath.

"Words, man! Words!" Kenneth exclaimed. "Simple words! Words make people think more than getting into a fight ever can. The words you read in a poem—or a song—burn in your mind," Kenneth said. "A fight—you forget about. But not *words.*"

Kenneth could feel ideas bursting into his brain. He gestured excitedly.

"You'll never forget the words," Kenneth continued. "Or at least the feelings they made you feel. So I think you should write the blues about it. And play them. For lots of people," Kenneth finished. He looked at Chauncey. Had he won? Had he convinced him?

"Yeah," Aleesa added. She stepped closer to Chauncey. "You should do that. Think about writing a blues song. It'll last forever. And if you fight, *you* probably won't last. There are just a few of us. And there are plenty of *them.* But your song—everyone will remember that. You can even play it for Langston," she said. She almost held her breath. Would Chauncey believe her? Would he believe Kenneth?

"That's a great idea," Ralph seconded. "You're a great blues writer."

Kenneth saw Chauncey's face begin to relax. The crease disappeared from between Chauncey's eyes. Chauncey shut his eyes for a moment. Then he drew a breath.

"Yeah," Chauncey said. "I—I guess you're right. Langston's right. Words really do work. I've seen it happen. For the common man too. Just as Langston says. Words really do make people face evil. I guess some people really *are* thinking about all of this hatred." He looked down at the ground. Then he looked over at the flags on the stage.

Aleesa followed his gaze. The U.S. flag hung on a standard in the still air. The state flag of North Carolina hung next to it. But so did the Confederate flag. Goose bumps rose on her arms. That flag had to go. And in her time, it would.

But plenty of words had to be written and sung before it would happen. Like "We Shall Overcome," she thought. She almost started humming it. She bit her lip.

"Maybe something like 'The Flag Blues,'" Chauncey said slowly, still staring at the flags.

"Well, then," Kenneth broke the silence. "Why don't you get started? You can play it for Langston. Maybe even tomorrow, if you finish it."

"I've got lots of ideas running around in my head," Chauncey admitted. He looked at the Bluesmen. "I think we'll come up with something pretty quick."

"Let's get started," Ralph urged. Together, the Bluesmen walked quickly up the aisle.

Just before they reached the exit, Chauncey stopped. "Hey," he called. "Thanks." He grinned.

"Whew!" Aleesa breathed. "We pulled that one off okay!" She leaned against the table. "I thought we might have a riot on our hands." She shut her eyes.

"What do you mean *we?*" Kenneth teased. "*I* was the one who thought of what to say to Chauncey." He grinned at Aleesa.

Aleesa made a face at him. "Okay," she snapped. "If you're so smart, then why aren't we back in Berkeley?" she taunted. She put her hands on her hips and tapped her foot.

"All right. All right," Kenneth grumbled. He began stacking books again. "I've been thinking a lot about it. And I still think we have to go to the UNC library, right here. That's the only thing I can think of. Unless we could get back to the Virginia Union Library. That's where we entered 1931, but I don't think we could get back to the library. So this may be our only hope," he admitted. He did hate to admit it too. What if it didn't work?

"What happens if we can't get back?" Aleesa began to wail. "Will we have to stay in the South? Or can we go with Langston? I don't like this at all. At *all!*"

Aleesa's voice echoed in the empty hall. Kenneth looked around. Thank goodness they were the only ones there. He frowned. "Shhhh! Just be quiet. As soon as the program is over tonight, let's go to the library. Okay?"

Aleesa turned the corners of her mouth down. "Fine. You'd just better be right," she said. "That's all I have to say."

Soon, hundreds of excited people filled Gerrard Hall. They laughed and talked together. Outside the doors, Kenneth saw the police. Their faces were grim. He hoped the police wouldn't need to do anything.

As always, as soon as Langston began reading, a hush fell over the audience. Aleesa and Kenneth smiled at each other. Aleesa gave Kenneth a thumbs-up sign.

The hypnotic tones of Langston's words wove a spell around the crowd. His voice rose and fell. He laughed with "Blues Fantasy." His voice softened with the speaker in "My People." He drew out the slow, rich tones of the words in "The Negro Speaks of Rivers." Finally, as he finished the final words of "I, Too, Sing America," the crowd leaped to its feet. Thunderous clapping vibrated in the air. People jumped on top of their seats, cheering.

"Holy smoke!" Kenneth said to Aleesa. "That's the best audience he's ever had! And there's been no trouble, either. Even with the *Contempo* article and poem. The crowd loves Langston."

"Yeah," Aleesa agreed. She gazed out at the crowd.

"And they're all colors too." She smiled. "It's almost like a look into the future," she said softly.

"Speaking of the future," Kenneth said, "let's get going to the library. I told Langston we had to look something up. The Bluesmen will clean up for us." He grabbed Aleesa's hand. Together they rushed up one of the aisles.

As they hurried out, they ran into the Bluesmen making their way down the aisle.

"Hey!" Chauncey called out. He was grinning. "We did it! We wrote a great blues piece. We've been jammin'. Wait until you hear it!"

"Langston's going to like it too," Ralph added. They raised their hands in good-byes.

"They were nice," Aleesa said regretfully. They raced past the columns and down the steps outside the hall. "Even if Chauncey was sort of a wild card," she said back over her shoulder to Kenneth.

"You're talking as if we're already back home in Berkeley," Kenneth scolded her. He caught up to her. "We don't know if this is going to work or not."

Gloom settled over Aleesa. Kenneth was right. She said a silent prayer. Please let them get home, she begged.

They rushed in the doors of the library. The librarian glanced up at them. "What are you doing here?" she asked, frowning. "We're about to close."

"We . . . ah . . . we're looking up something for

Langston Hughes," Kenneth said. "You know, the poet?"

The librarian's frown vanished. "Oh, of course," she said. "I wish I'd been able to hear him tonight. He's a wonderful poet. But I had to work." She motioned to the dozens of shelves. "Help yourself. Let me know if I can help," she added.

"What was the call number for Langston?" Aleesa asked in a whisper. "Wasn't it 811?"

"You're right," Kenneth said. "Are you thinking what I'm thinking? If we recreate what happened, it'll work? If we let some books fall on our heads?" he asked.

Aleesa grinned. "Yeah," she said. They peered around shelves. They walked quickly down the rows and rows of books.

"There!" Aleesa crowed. She grabbed Kenneth's arm and tugged him between two rows.

The Weary Blues, Kenneth read from the book cover. He smiled. "Look—there are no other books. He hasn't written them yet!" he said.

"Are you ready?" Aleesa asked. Her mouth felt dry. Was this going to work? She rubbed the top of her head. It was probably going to hurt too.

"Uh-huh," Kenneth agreed. "Shut your eyes." He reached up to the top shelf. He swept the books off. He winced.

Thud! Bam! Crash! Thump! A dozen books tumbled from the shelf, showering Kenneth and Aleesa.

"Oweeee!" Aleesa howled. She grabbed her head

with her hands. "You didn't have to get so rambunctious," she complained.

Then everything went black. Bright spots came and went behind her eyelids. Aleesa slumped to the floor. "I—I'm dizzy," she moaned.

"Aaaargh," Kenneth exclaimed. "I think I got carried away!" He rubbed his head and shut his eyes. Red flashes burst behind his eyelids. He dropped to his knees on the library floor. "Ooooh, I'm gonna have a lump on my head after this," he said. "The room's going around," he said. The shelves reeled and blurred.

"Hey!" Aleesa exclaimed. She opened her eyes. She looked down. No dress. Jeans were in its place!

"I'm not wearing a dress!" she crowed. "Yes! We're back!" She looked at Kenneth. "And you're as ugly as you ever were!" she teased.

Kenneth looked around them. It had to be, didn't it? Wasn't it the familiar Berkeley library that surrounded them? Yes! he thought in relief. A couple of scraggly-looking students frowned at them. The hippies were still here. This was definitely the University of California Library at Berkeley!

Aleesa bent down and picked up her backpack. She turned over one of the books on the floor.

"Look!" she said. She held it up for Kenneth to see. "It's called *Black Misery* by Langston Hughes. It's a kids' book. He wrote this just before he died in 1967. That's why we didn't hear him read it aloud." She riffled through the pages. "You know what?" she asked. "I think we're going to have a lot to say in our project. Langston would be proud of us."

An idea burst into Kenneth's brain. He hid a smile. He'd get Aleesa now.

"Huh? What project?" Kenneth asked. He'd see if he could scare Aleesa just one more time. "And what do you mean, Langston would be proud of us?" he asked, trying to sound casual. "What in the world are you talking about, anyway?" He pretended to look worried. "Are you okay? Did something happen to you?"

Aleesa stood stock still. What was wrong with Kenneth? Had she dreamed the whole adventure with Langston Hughes? Was she crazy? Her heart began to pound. She gripped the Langston Hughes book tightly.

"Don't . . . don't you remember—?" Aleesa began to stammer. Then she saw Kenneth's mouth twitch.

"You rat!" Aleesa squawked. She whacked him with the book. "That'll teach you! You almost gave me a heart attack!"

Kenneth laughed. He held his hands up. "Okay, okay," he chuckled. "Back off! I just wanted to give you a hard time. You're the one who wasn't so sure about poetry, remember?"

Aleesa made a face. "Yeah? Well, that's changed." Then a smile began to creep across her face. "We'll change the class too. We'll show them what words can really do," she said.

"Sounds great," Kenneth agreed.

"And we'll show them how poetry really can be for—" Aleesa began. She paused, waiting for Kenneth to join in.

"The common man," Kenneth said with a grin as they finished Langston's sentence together.

Langston Hughes

Langston Hughes broke the mold of the poet. He was the first black poet to write about being black. He was also the first black poet to write for the average black person, not just highly educated blacks. Because of that, his poetry made some people angry.

Langston Hughes wrote the way people really talked. His subjects were often the lives of everyday black people. He believed black writers should be proud of being black and not try to write as if they were another color. He hoped that writing well about blacks would bring about respect, justice, and equality.

Langston Hughes was born February 1, 1902, in Joplin, Missouri. His parents separated when he was a baby. His father, James Hughes, moved to Mexico and bought a huge ranch. Langston stayed with his grandmother, Mary Langston, while his mother moved different places looking for work.

SHATTER WITH WORDS: LANGSTON HUGHES

Mary Langston was a proud woman. She was the first black woman to go to Oberlin College. She taught Langston to have pride in his family.

One of Langston's uncles was acting president of Howard University and was elected to Congress. Both of Mary Langston's husbands were well known for their educations and their strong characters. They fought for black rights.

Langston's grandmother died when he was 13. Langston went to live with friends of his grandmother's, the Reeds.

Langston loved the magical world of movies. In elementary school, he wrote poetry during recess. Church activities like dramas and poetry readings fed his imagination. The Reeds took him to Kansas City where he first heard the blues. It seemed like a wonderful new language to him.

Langston was elected to the student council in high school. He was editor of the yearbook. And he lettered in track.

When Langston had completed high school, he knew he wanted to become a writer.

While Langston was visiting his father in Mexico, he got several poems published. He was only 19. One famous poem was called "The Negro Speaks of Rivers."

Langston enrolled in Columbia University in New York City. He wanted to be near Harlem. He'd lived all his life in mostly white towns and went to school with white children. And now he wanted to feel like he belonged somewhere.

The exciting life in Harlem made Langston happy. He loved the jazz, the blues, and the friendliness.

But college life was different. Langston suffered because of the color of his skin.

After one year, he dropped out and found a job working on a steamer. He traveled to Europe, writing poems all the time. Langston spent some time in Paris, washing dishes at a jazz cafe. He loved the music and the rhythms. Listening to jazz and blues, he tried to write poetry that had a beat like music. He kept sending poems back to the United States. More poems were published.

At 23, Langston sailed back to New York. When he got to Harlem, he found he was famous. People loved his poems.

Langston knew he was finally ready for college. Because a rich lady had read Langston's published poetry and liked it, she offered to pay for his college. Langston went to Lincoln University, a black university in Pennsylvania. By now, the *New York Times* had already called him "a poet of promise." He was only 25.

Langston won an important poetry prize. It was the Harmon Gold Award for Distinguished Black Literature. Langston graduated from college. With the $400 he won, he went to Cuba for a year.

When Langston came back to the U.S., he went on a poetry reading tour through the South. He was determined to make money from poetry. Langston wanted to prove there was an audience for black poetry.

After that, Langston Hughes made his living as a writer. He wrote many poems, books, and plays. Langston Hughes always wrote about the real lives of blacks. He tried to write with the feeling of the blues and of jazz rhythm. He wrote about being proud to be black. He wrote how life was good. He also wrote about the hard times, because he believed if people had to look at the evil around them, they would have to think about it. If they thought about it, they could change.

Even when people treated him badly because of his color, Langston didn't get angry. He knew he was better than they were. He always kept his sense of humor. One of his most famous poems is "Life is Fine." That poem expresses how Langston felt about life.

Langston also lectured in schools and colleges. He encouraged young black men and women to become writers. One writer he encouraged was Margaret Walker.

Langston won many honors. He was given an honorary Ph.D. from Lincoln University. He received a Guggenheim Fellowship and a Rosenwald Fellowship.

Langston Hughes wrote sixteen books of poems, two novels, three collections of short stories, twenty plays, children's poetry, musicals and operas, three autobiographies, and dozens of magazine articles and radio and TV scripts. He also edited anthologies of black writers, hoping to make them popular.

Langston Hughes died of cancer on May 22, 1967. His apartment was given landmark status by New York City. The Queens Borough Public Library started the Langston Hughes Community Library and Cultural Center. Here, people can see all of his works as well as the largest Black Heritage reading collection in New York City.

Langston was proud to be black and had a gift of writing. His writing helped others to believe in themselves. He did much for the pride of black people. He will always be remembered for the way he communicated strong feelings and ideas to people of all colors. He hoped that his writing would lead eventually to freedom and justice.